Quakeland

Quakeland

Francesca Lia Block

Manic D Press
San Francisco

for
the Spirits

Cover painting: *Still a Tadpole, Already a Frog* by Irene Hardwicke Olivieri

Library of Congress Cataloging in Publication Data

Block, Francesca Lia.
Quakeland / Francesca Lia Block.
 p. cm.
 ISBN 978-1-945665-30-1 (paperback) 978-1-933149-49-3 (ebook)
1. Women--Fiction. 2. Interpersonal relations--Fiction. 3. Los Angeles (Calif.)--Fiction. 4. Psychological fiction. I. Title.
 PS3552.L617Q35 2008
 813'.54--dc22

 2007052533

Contents

Quakeland

QUAKELAND
August 21, 2005

Who knows how much of this is me and how much is where I live and have lived for my entire life? Such a green flowering desert between the snow queen's mountains and the surf demon's sea. A hemispheric light that gilds your skin like gold-leaf foil. Such a city—you wouldn't imagine that it is supposed to fall into the ocean at any moment, that even the sun is a carcinogen; you wouldn't think that there is anything to fear.

They might as well call it "Quakeland" but I guess that could affect the burgeoning real estate. Angels sell and if this scarlet starlet harlot ho knows one thing, it is how to sell herself.

I got an e-mail once, from a disaster expert, saying that you aren't supposed to go under doorways or furniture during an earthquake. You can be crushed, as Mr. Disaster said, "to the thickness of your bones." You're supposed to duck and cover next to a large, soft piece of furniture like a couch and trust in something called "a triangle of life." This is the safe space left next to objects when the building collapses.

Disaster Man, I am Quakeland born and raised; you have to believe in a safe space first.

THE TOWER
September 10, 2001

A jester marionette bobs his head and moves his wooden jaw open and shut, open and shut. Airplanes are flying out of his monkey mouth into the side of a building that looks like the Tower card in the classic Tarot deck. An acid yellow skeleton structure spewing flame and bodies.

I hear these words: "This is the fool who brought the world as we know it to its end."

TRIAGE
September 20, 2001

I didn't even recognize the writing. I could hardly make it out and when I did, I didn't remember the dream. It was as if someone else had it, wrote it down. And the person that did have the dream seemed more alive than me.

Kali said that many psychics mentally visited the actual site, the ruins of the twin buildings, after it happened and comforted and guided all the desolate souls who weren't able to leave yet. It was like handing them a cell phone to make the last call, a piece of paper and a pen to write the last note, Kali said. Some resolution. Psychic triage. I don't know how to do that. All I have is the vision, the apocalypse.

"Many more people died from government nuclear testing in the desert," said Kali. "You can look it up on line. No one talks about that."

Grace said, "Write it down in your journal, keep writing them down if you have another, that's what helps Gerald when he has a bad dream."

Of course, his don't come true. And Gerald has Grace the rescuer beside him, when he is nightmaring in the dark.

How do I tell you how much I love Grace? How she brought me back from the dead? How she is the best mom in the world? How she is the best dancer not only because of her training, but because of how much joy she expresses and how much she gives to her partner?

This is all I can say: When threatened to be taken from you, love is the worst earthquake I know. It can crush you to the thickness of your bones. Love can be a tumor sometimes. Terminal. It can make you vomit. It can make you want to cut it out. It can take you over against your will.

GRACELAND
February 14, 2003

Grace and I are walking up through a terraced garden of bird of paradise and naked lady flowers, massive mythic stone creatures and crumbling fountains, to a very old mansion. This is where we live. There is a giant ballroom with a parquet floor and mirrored walls. There is a dining room with a long table set with plates of whipped cream-covered Belgian waffles and glasses of wine and candles in tall silver holders. In the nursery, there are china dolls, bigger than real five-year-olds, with pale blue glass eyes and wigs of real hair. Two young children are playing with some plastic toy soldiers.

And… the soldiers are moving by themselves, marching out the door.

"Where are they going?" I ask.

"To war," Grace says in a small, salty voice.

I see that the children are dressed in army fatigues. They are marching out the door too, following the little plastic men. We can't stop them.

DEATH BY WATER
December 23, 2004

Severed chunks bobbing in the sea. Huge feet and hands, limbs and elongated heads with blank snake eyes and grim mouths. Totems. On the shore sits a dark-haired woman with huge earrings tugging down her lobes. When I look closely I can see that the large white orbs are the sun-bleached, polished skulls of children.

There is a feeling of compression in my chest and I know something has come and something even worse is on its way.

TSUNAMI MAN

Katrina had been too wary to go before—one hundred and fifty barefoot people dancing ecstatically, crawling on the floor, weeping, climbing over each other. But the day after the tsunami, Grace insisted.

"No wonder you're depressed, man," Grace said, in that warm, hoarse little voice. "You never leave your house except to go to work. No wonder you need Zoloft. I would die if I didn't shake it off every week."

Grace beat melanoma twice, using Western medicine, herbs, acupuncture, a vegan diet and her dancing. And love, she said. "I don't care if it sounds too new age fey." For her husband, Gerald, and her twins and Katrina. Sarah and Benji were born after the second bout but Grace said she's always carried them around inside her heart. Katrina had dreamed them, too. The soldier dream before the war.

Sarah and Benji both had blond curls, round eyes, long eyelashes, cherub cheeks. Their faces looked exactly alike. In spite of their obviously different genders, people continually asked if they were identical twins, and then winced with embarrassment, "Oh, of course not, what was I thinking?"

Grace and Gerald's kids looked nothing like Grace, except for their coloring, and even less like Gerald. Grace said she couldn't believe they came out of her body. Of course, Katrina knew they did. She was there.

It was hard to see Grace in pain but her face was so lit up that Katrina knew it was okay. Sarah came easily, just slid right out. Her eyes were open, it seemed, right away, and so were her little hands. Her feet were pointed, like a ballerina's. Benji struggled longer; he was bigger and Grace said she felt like he wasn't sure he wanted to be in the world. Like he knew how sad things could get. But Sarah was a fighter. Even though she was smaller she always acted as if she were trying to protect him — the way she tossed her arm across his chest when they slept and cried louder than he did when he hurt himself.

Sarah was round-faced and curly but it was obvious she was her mother's daughter when you watched her dance. She was the Sugar Plum Fairy in her ballet class recital, poised on her tiptoes the whole time, while the other little girls followed her around, holding up her tulle train. People marveled at her. "A natural," they said. "It runs in the family."

Benji already had the muscled arms and legs and tapering torso of a miniature athlete. He insisted on wearing a cape to school everyday. He pointed his fingers in front of his face and made whooshing sounds with his lips. "I'm Piderman!" Grace, the pacifist, insisted that he was not making a weapon but protecting people from bad guys with his superpowers. When Grace's parents gave him a huge bag of plastic soldiers for his birthday she didn't get them out of his hands in time. As a last resort she invented a game called "We want to go home!" until she could subtly make them disappear by the handful into the trash.

"Where are my sholdiers?," he demanded.

"They went home to the people they love," she said, handing him a box of eight fifteen-dollar-a-piece wooden trains with inane, smiling faces, each different enough to make a child want all seventy-five of them.

"I think it's time to find you a man," Grace told Katrina on the day of the tsunami, because disaster precognition was a hard thing to accept.

Katrina didn't want to think about the dream either but she knew she was in trouble when it came to men. The week before, she was trying to make a rhyme for the kids at her pre-school; all she could come up with was the unusable:

Miss Mousey had a housey
She lived there all alone
Until she found a spousey
And then she had a home
Mousey and her spousey
Had babies one, two, three
And only then in their warm den
Was there a family

The only men she ever saw besides Gerald and the dads who brought their kids to school, were the ones she paid or coaxed in to visit. The bubble man who encased the children in giant individual soap bubbles. The firemen who brought their shiny red engine for the kids to explore. The reptile guy that had six of them stand in a row to hold a giant white snake. Only the reptile didn't wear a thick band on his left ring finger but he was the same shocking white color as the snake and seemed much more interested in his lizards than in Katrina.

There were also men at Kali's yoga class, but they were all there to worship Kali.

"Yes," said Kali, on the day of the tsunami, closing her sunflower-center eyes, "I feel someone coming."

Katrina wore black to feel thinner. She wore her long brown hair loose around her shoulders, instead of in the usual ponytail, and her best pink lip gloss. The delicate, dark-rimmed glasses were tucked into their case; without them her eyes looked greener. She thought if she danced hard enough she might forget that she had dreamed of another disaster before it had occurred.

She and Grace were dancing in front of the altar with the pre-tsunami beach postcard pictures from Southeast Asia when he came up. Tall and slim in prayer beads and a light blue shirt that matched his eyes. His beautifully-shaped head was shaved. He had those high cheekbones and a flash of smile. The large, heart-shaped red birthmark on the side of his face looked beautiful, not aberrant. You wouldn't have thought there was anything to fear.

The three of them were flinging themselves around, all limbs and sweat. He had an almost feline grace for such a big man. When Grace waved her arms in flowing rainbow silk and let her blond hair fall out of its braid, fall freely around her shoulders, (thin hair, naturally golden, always scrupulously clean) he whooped. Katrina spun until she was dizzy.

At the end of class everyone held hands and formed a circle. The man was next to Katrina. A tall, thin woman with tilted blue-green eyes and big breasts was on the other side of him. He smiled at both of them, shifting his head back and forth.

"Jasper," he announced when it was his turn to say his name. Like the stone. Katrina tried to think what color it was.

She had some pink petals left in her purse from the roses she had put on the altar to acknowledge the tsunami victims. She took them out, rubbing the thick, almost powdery silkiness. Just then she turned and he was standing there, smiling boyishly, holding out a flyer for a yoga workshop. Up close, his irises had very small pupils and a faraway look. This close, not moving, seen from below, he was taller even than she'd thought.

He took the petals and crushed them, then sniffed his fingers.

"I'm Jasper."

"I know. Katrina."

"Thank you for the petals," he said, and then he was gone.

She wondered for a moment if he were another of those hit-and-run L.A. angels. Her car had broken down in the middle of the highway three times and someone had always come out of nowhere to push it to the side of the road. She remembered them vividly. One was a huge, bald African with astonishing diamonds in his ears. One looked like a Latino gang member with muscular, completely tattoo-covered, flowery arms and a baby face. The third had tumbling black curls, white skin, a gap between his front teeth and blue eyes. As soon as she was safe, they had disappeared. Kali said they were Los Angeles angels. Katrina wondered why they couldn't have stayed a little longer but Kali said that's how angels are.

This one was different, though. He hadn't rescued her from her nightmares. Not yet. And although he, too, had vanished into the ether, a flyer with his email address on it was in her hand.

SHRINK RAP

The Zoloft had started to work. All dreams had stopped. She wasn't gritting her teeth at night. Her jaw stopped aching. When she looked in the mirror she didn't just stand there scrutinizing, pinching parts of her body. She just put on some lipstick and walked away.

It fascinated her how such a little pill could do so much. What was it in her brain that made her call herself fat? What did the pill actually do to shut the voice up? And without the voice what would she allow herself to do with her life? What choices would be different? She knew she wouldn't have gone dancing with Grace if she weren't on the meds. She wouldn't have gone dancing and she wouldn't have met Jasper.

There were side effects. She was never hungry. Her stomach had curled itself into a fist but she wasn't losing weight. She phoned the psychiatrist who had prescribed the medication and asked him about the appetite loss.

"You should be happy," he droned. "Most people gain weight on SSRIs. Carbohydrate cravings."

Great.

"And the dreams?" he asked, uncomfortable, coughing slightly. She could tell he didn't believe they were pre-cognition, just a sign of a chemical disorder.

Although she didn't dream, she didn't sleep very well either.

She woke at three in the morning — often drenched through with sweat — and had to force herself to stay in bed until five. Then she'd scurry around the house dusting, sweeping, watering, rearranging. She was tired at school, but she had been before, and now she wasn't wracked with the nightmares all day. And her house was clean.

She couldn't come. The curse of the SSRI miracle drug. Other people reported low libido but her desire was still there. She just couldn't respond. Her fingers fumbled for hours, body almost peaking, never quite. Until she finally gave up with exhaustion.

Another side effect was listed on the package insert: *possible suicidal thoughts*.

It was still worth it to be on the vitamin Z, as Kali called it. Kali didn't believe in anti-depressants, though; she thought it was best to face everything head on, but Katrina knew she needed them. Needed to stop walking around all day in a living-dead daze, sick from dreams.

And maybe she could come if an actual man touched her, though she'd never been that easily orgasmic, even before. And what man would be patient enough? Kali had told her that the fickle female orgasm insured the choice of a good mate. But based on what Katrina had seen, it seemed to insure frustration more than anything else.

The psychiatrist said, "Most people find a little lowering of the libido is a small price to pay in exchange for the benefits to the rest of their lives. And it seems that the, shall we say, almost masculine intensity of your sex drive might have been ultimately destructive for you."

Katrina wondered if she could stop seeing him. She'd had a worse history with therapists than she did with boyfriends, and each relationship had a corresponding shrink.

Marcus — a sweet, gentle English major who wore tie-dye — brought her wildflowers and wrote her lovely, inscrutable poetry. But she was so homesick and worried about the lump in her mother's breast that everything made her cry. Marcus just got more and more bewildered and withdrawn. The counselor Katrina saw didn't seem to have anything to say; he kept falling asleep during the sessions. She brought in some collages she'd done—women with flowers or winged insects for breasts, and see-through, empty pregnant bellies—thinking they might give him some insight, or at least keep him awake, and they dripped rose petals and glitter all over his office. His eyes did open for a moment; he grimaced and suggested she put the things in plastic so they wouldn't shed. When she called him collect from a hospital in Los Angeles to tell him her mother had died, he asked her to dial direct the next time.

After graduation, she was living with Tommy, an androgynous goth singer and guitar player from San Francisco. (*Why do all rock singers seem to have names that end in Y?* she wondered. Was it a sign that they couldn't seem to grow up or something more sinister? Y as in why.) He came home late at night after band practice. She cried the whole time they were making love.

When she told the psychiatrist she had found that she felt jealous almost all the time his eyebrows went up; he leaned forward as if he were making some kind of interesting discovery about an insect under his microscope.

"And how does this manifest?"

She explained that the feeling was so strong the only thing she could compare it to was some kind of disaster. As if when her boyfriend flirted with other women, or when she even imagined him flirting, she was literally dying. She used the word "Holocaust" and the man's eyebrows went up even more.

"And how do you think this fits in with your early childhood experiences?"

She talked about her dad leaving and the psychiatrist nodded, pressing the tips of his fingers together. Katrina could almost see the cold vaporizing off his skin like dry ice.

"It sounds as if this trauma manifests as your fear of men leaving at any time. There are medications that can take the edge off enough for us to explore this."

"Actually, I think I was Anne Frank in another life," she said, and left, and never came back.

Tommy moved back up North, and after awhile Katrina met Jake, an up-and-coming visual artist with a goatee and a house in Silverlake, who told her she was way too possessive and if she wanted to keep seeing him she'd have to find a good shrink. First she saw a man who spent a good portion of each session discussing the beautiful actresses who came to see him and that even they had feelings of insecurity about their perfect bodies. Her next therapist—the best one—died from a rare disease. Quickly, the way Katrina's mother had. The therapist never even told Katrina she was ill. And her family was in such shock that no one called to tell Katrina about the death. There was only a note on the woman's office door.

Finally, Katrina broke up with Jake when she found out he officially considered himself a polyamorist. She hadn't even heard the word before. It wasn't even in the spellcheck on her computer.

After she and her next boyfriend, Daniel—a shy high school English teacher—got pregnant, miscarried and stopped touching each other, they went to an attractive young counselor who told Katrina that neither she nor the therapist herself were the most beautiful women in the world but that they could still lead fulfilling, happy lives, and that diets and even plastic surgery were viable options on the road to self-love. At one point the therapist spoke to Daniel in private. Then she told Katrina, "I can't reveal what he said, but there was a lot of sexual content, not necessarily about you. He's still sexual. If you do some work on yourself, the relationship might have a chance." When Katrina told her she felt betrayed, the woman said, "I see you are a deeply angry person. I've done so much for you and now you are projecting your upset with him onto me. I see this as really callus behavior and I don't feel I can keep seeing you."

The Zoloft that the latest psychiatrist prescribed was better than all of them.

She wondered why she had chosen the therapists and the men so badly, not seeing they were only the fun-house mirror reflections of her own stricken self.

LISE MARIA GARDNER   MAY 6, 1950 - MAY 1, 1992
May 1, 1992

I see the digital clock, the one she and I bought on Hollywood Boulevard the week before I moved up north. Three-thirty, it says. The time when, statistically, the most people die.

The phone was ringing and it wasn't until then that I woke up from the dream and opened my eyes. Three-thirty, the clock said. I heard Uncle Carl and I knew.

Marcus gave me a ride to the airport and Uncle Carl picked me up and drove me to the hospital. I think I had imagined being in bed with her when it happened, holding her hand, stroking her face. I would have shaved her head for her. Given her a scalp treatment and a pedicure. But instead she was in a coma in this hospital in the Valley. Just this white sculpture of my mother in the hospital bed. She was already gone. I shouldn't have gone back to school like she begged me. I should have dropped out and stayed with her. Or at least gone home for her birthday.

Things come back to you. Not what you'd expect, not what you'd say at a memorial service. Like eating cold pizza for breakfast, blueberry buckwheat pancakes for dinner. Crocheting sweaters for the cats and using their paw prints to decorate our handmade pottery. Agreeing on art house movies and exhibits at the museum, sharing the same taste in clothes. How she bought me condoms when I was sixteen. "Not that I'm telling you it's okay; this is just in case you find someone you really love." Like not needing a best friend, because she was it. I guess you could say that at a memorial service. That was a mistake, though, the best friend thing. Because I never tried hard to make any and now she is gone and I am really alone except for Marcus. I should go back to him in Santa Cruz but I don't want to leave Mom's house in the canyon. I don't want to leave this ugly city that she managed to love. "If you pick your routes, it's paradise," she'd say. "Only take the canyons, never the freeways. And travel at the off-hours. Mediate at the Self-Realization Fellowship. Do yoga. Eat picnics on the beach. Hike in the mountains. Ride the carousel as often as possible. Be kind to everyone but only associate with those you love." Marcus has no tolerance for this city. He's a Santa Cruz man in his Grateful Dead shirt. But look at me, Miss Goth, I don't belong there.

Most women pick men who remind them of their fathers. Since I never knew mine, I keep looking for my mom in a man's body. I guess that is too much to ask.

I suppose that unlike heart failure and car wrecks, cancer prepares you for the loss but in another way it feels worse. Like I have been grieving for years but, really, the grieving has just begun.

NEVERLAND

She took all the money she'd saved from the sale of her mother's house and opened a pre-school. She called it "Neverland," hoping that parents wouldn't hesitate to send their children somewhere named after a place where no one grew up, but everyone seemed to like it. Who wanted to grow up anyway?

Neverland was in a Victorian gingerbread house with a big porch and an enclosed yard. It was painted with pastel colors. The children had planted a vegetable garden and a flower garden. They had made a fairy bower and built a fairy city in the mud. There were bunny rabbits running around on the lawn. The kitchen smelled of fresh baked bread or cookies. The children's artwork covered the walls and hung from the ceiling. Paper leaves, pumpkins, Christmas trees, dreidels, snowflakes, Valentine hearts, spring flowers, Easter eggs, suns, moons, and stars. In the winter Katrina hired someone to make fake snow and Gerald dressed up as Santa Claus. In the spring, the children drew on eggs with crayons and then dipped them in bright bowls of dye and Grace dressed up as the Easter Bunny. Music was always playing. Lots of Bach that was supposed to help the kids' brains develop and *Puff the Magic Dragon* that made all the parents cry when

"Jackie Paper came no more...
"Dragons live forever but not so little boys."

Twenty-five children from the ages of two-and-a-half to five, including Sarah and Benji, came to Neverland every day. Katrina and her assistants changed diapers, applied band-aids, read stories, and set out art supplies and puzzles and blocks and dress-up clothes and dolls. The children called her Teacher Kitty Kat, made her pictures, and let her hold them when they were sad but, of course, when their parents came at the end of the day, they were too excited to even say good-bye to her.

It was not the same as having a baby of her own, but it helped.

It might even have been enough, if not for the wave.

CONTACT

The studio was different at night. Katrina moved around by herself in the dim light, easier in her body than usual. Not worrying about the size of her hips. She closed her eyes and rippled her spine in front of the altar. She had brought stargazer lilies. A little of the rusty pollen from the stamens had already stained her white T-shirt.

Grace was home with Gerald and the kids so Katrina danced by herself. Wishing for Grace. She knew she probably looked like a crazy person. It was a relief to be dancing in a room full of people who didn't care. Even without her glasses she easily recognized Jasper sauntering in. A surge of energy rushed through her body. He came over and took her hand. They danced playfully together for a while and then when the music got faster she broke away. She felt so much intensity, like some kind of tidal wave of her own. It was hard to contain it.

Finally, she collapsed near the wall.

He slid down next to her. "How are you?"

"I'm okay. It feels like my life is changing."

He nodded. "Mine, too."

They sat side by side, gazing straight ahead at the dancers. Katrina could feel him turn his head to look at her.

"You're so familiar. You look like my ex-girlfriend, actually. Esther. She was the love of my life. Different from the others."

"What happened?"

He seemed distracted, dreaming off into the crowd of dancers. "Oh. It's a long story. Maybe she was just there to help me recognize you."

She found that she was leaning against his arm as if she'd known him for a long time. His body felt so comfortable. Warm and strong but light.

Someone announced, "Let this next dance be a prayer for the victims of the tsunami."

Jasper stood up. He offered his hand and pulled her to her feet. She'd seen couples doing this thing, this "contact dance," as they called it, the day she met him. It confused her at first. She thought those people were lovers; it looked so intimate, sexy and intense. Sometimes they just stood there, facing each other, touching each other's eyelids and cheekbones and lips. But it was just a dance.

Isn't it all?

Jasper had her hands at first, moving her around gently, smiling at her, meeting her gaze with his. Then his hand was at her lower back, this warm pressure and he was steering her; she felt so light, not bulky or too big the way she usually did. He spun her, flung her, he lifted her, supported her on his back like she was weightless. Her spine was a flexible flower stem. There was no fear. No worry that she was too heavy for him, that he couldn't hold her. She dropped her head back so her hair touched the floor.

"You're brave," he whispered.

She wondered what that meant and why she trusted him so much.

Jasper's legs were between hers. She was wet. Wishing that the Zoloft had taken away desire with the orgasm—it wasn't fair. Anorgasmia. She knew she'd be up struggling with her body all night long.

Jasper's hands grazed under her breasts and her nipples

hardened.

She heard him moan, "You are so hot. My God!"

Five years. Forget dancing. Five years since she'd had sex with a man.

Jasper picked her up and spun her around, her head thrown back, one leg pointed to the sky.

It felt as if they knew each other's bodies so well. She had no fear or hesitation. She remembered reading once, in some women's magazine, that intense motion can make you think you were falling in love.

He was a roller coaster ride. He was a tidal wave.

"See," she said. "I told you my life was changing."

"Katrina, I have to go."

Before it really registered in her head, she was watching him walk out the door. Suddenly she remembered why they had been dancing—all those people killed by that apocalyptic wave. The medication she was on had taken most of her tears but there were a few left.

DREAM MAN
November 13, 2004

A crowd of people—all shouting, dancing around a fire in the center of a large room that looks like a high school gymnasium. The women are bare breasted and I feel ashamed that I can't be free enough to take off my shirt. An effigy in a hat and coat hangs over the fire. I walk outside, away from the suffocating smoke. There is a man standing there, his head turned, face eager, as if he has been waiting for me. He has huge hands like a puppet's dangling from his wrists and a snake around his neck. There is a heart painted on his face.

GODDESSES AND GHOSTS

"I feel like my life is changing." Why had she said that? It was so embarrassing. It told him how much she liked him. *But it was true, wasn't it?* Nothing to do with Jasper; her life was in transition. She was moving out of the studio apartment she'd been in for ten years. It was in a stucco and glass U-shaped building with a pool. The courtyard smelled of chlorine and bleach. Rose in Palms was a street lined with apartments, frayed-looking palm trees but no roses to speak of. Mostly college students and very few families lived there. Moving trucks parked at the curb almost every weekend

Where she was going felt semi-permanent and grown up. A place she might be able to have a family some day.

It was the house Grace and Gerald had lived in, where they had conceived Sarah and Benji.

The landlady was happy because Katrina knew Grace, but the picture of the dogs helped the most. A lot of people wouldn't even talk to you if you were renting with pets. This lady had a little boneless Pekinese named Cookie who sat in Katrina's lap during the interview.

"What angels," she said when Katrina showed her the picture of Bilbo and Frodo, and told her they had both been strays who showed up at her doorstep.

"I just have to run a credit check and then I think it's yours," the woman said. "You can move in in two weeks."

The house was only a few blocks from a park. Katrina could walk her dogs around the rectangle of shiny lawn, under the shady trees. She could even walk them there at night because there were always girls' soccer teams or couples playing tennis under extra bright street lamps. On the Fourth of July you could see fireworks from your picnic blanket on the grass. On Halloween, there was a haunted house, with cobwebs and ghouls, peeled-grape eyeballs and cold spaghetti intestines, set up in the stone building at the edge of the park. At Christmas you could eat pancakes with Santa. And at Easter you could hunt for plastic eggs full of candy in the grass.

The house was tiny and run-down but it had lots of windows all around and French doors. Light just swept through. There were wooden floors, white walls. Tile was important—not so much the quality—it could be chipped, cracked—as the color. She'd turned down perfectly good apartments because of nasty brown and orange tile. The kitchen tile was yellow and white, and the bathroom aqua green. And the house had a garden with roses and irises and geraniums and jasmine and honeysuckle growing up the fence. Morning glories and bougainvillea entwined in the trees and on the phone wires. There was even a rickety old tree house.

There was a ghost. She hadn't seen him but Kali had. He was outside the green glass window box. A garden spirit, Kali said, tall and willowy, wearing some kind of hat. He was very loving, very peaceful, though a little lonely. He loved the house, Kali said, and would be glad that Katrina was moving in. She was glad he was there, too.

Kali said that some people believed there weren't any ghosts left on this plane anymore. She said that these people believed that what we still called "ghosts" were actually ascendant beings. *I'll take that*, Katrina thought.

When Grace first told her they were buying a house in Venice, Katrina imagined moving into this one. She would fill the rooms with teak from Thailand, pale beaded Indian fabrics, star-gazers and goddess statues.

Kali told Katrina it was important to have statues of the goddess. They were all over Kali's studio. Katrina went there to get a free massage after Kali had accidentally dislocated one of her ribs. Katrina was in Kali's yoga class and Kali was pushing on her back, trying to get her to open her heart, she said. All of a sudden they heard a popping sound. It hurt like hell, a breathless slam of pain. Later, Katrina told herself the pain was worth it. It was what led her to become closer to Kali.

Kali was half Mexican, one-quarter African, and one-quarter Swedish. She had a little Native American in there, too, she said, although it had crossed Katrina's mind that almost every healer in town made the same claim. Men's jaws came unhinged when Kali walked into a room, but what made her especially beautiful to Katrina was how her eyes looked sad and tired under her perfectly arched brows, like she'd been through shit. All she'd told Katrina was that she'd gone crazy, had a complete breakdown, that it was something with men, a man. And then once she was dancing in this goddess workshop with a real snake wrapped around her shoulders. The snake put its face into her face and stared into her eyes.

"That's when I felt the Goddess," she said. "It changed everything. Now I don't put so much into the men. It's all about Her work. And my friends. Even the idea of infidelity doesn't scare me at all."

She'd gotten two snake tattoos, one wreathing her bicep, the other low around her hips, as a reminder.

Because Grace was taken, Katrina imagined living with Kali in a house filled with goddesses carved from semi-precious stones. The women would always have fresh flowers and candles and incense burning on the altar. Dancing rituals and feasts in the garden. They might even raise a baby together, she thought, if no man came along.

"You have the traditional goddess body," Kali said. "The earth girl body. It's lovely."

When Katrina came to her studio for the massage she closed the door behind them and whispered, "No one knows we are here."

She had lit candles everywhere and the burnt umber walls glowed. There was a strong scent of lavender oil. While Kali massaged her, Katrina babbled the whole time about wanting a man and a house. She said, "I know it's not spiritually correct, though."

Kali laughed. She looked feral, revealing her tiny, wicked teeth.

"Oh well. Let's not be spiritually correct. Let's just ask Her anyway."

I guess it worked, Katrina thought. She had Grace's house. And she had met Jasper.

The rib Kali had dislocated had healed. Mostly. Sometimes Katrina felt a twinge there, behind the heart she was trying to open.

REALLY SUPER BEAUTIFUL
July 4, 1992

I finally dragged my big ass off the couch to a dance class again. It was pretty humiliating. I mean the last time I danced seriously was when I was sixteen at summer camp in Idyllwild. I'm so out of shape it's pathetic. But Dr. Carter seems to think it's a good idea and that's about the only advice he's given to me that I actually agree with so... Anyway, I would have probably left before the class was over and never come back except there was this woman there. Really super beautiful with long blond hair like some kind of angel. Those rare light green eyes. And an incredible dancer. So grounded but buoyant at the same time. When it was time to go across the floor she saw the expression of horror on my face and waited with me. She whispered, "Follow me," and we went together. It helped so much to watch her. When class was over she grinned and introduced herself.

It's the first time since Mom's been gone that I haven't spent the whole evening lying on the couch eating ice cream and feeling my breasts for lumps. I actually took myself to a movie and dinner. Just like if she were still here.

I dream about Grace. Her veins are vines. She has red roses sprouting out of her skin. The roses seem sinister, devouring, rather than symbols of love and beauty and I want to keep her safe.

CHAKRAS

The studio had a mural of a four-armed goddess seated on a lotus in a river, a blue god playing a flute to a cow on the bank and a god with the head of an elephant. Rain fell melodically on the skylight. There were mostly women there, women about Katrina's age or younger. She wondered how many of them had received the flyer from Jasper at dances.

Jasper met her eyes when she walked in the room but he didn't give her any special attention. He was calm and almost kingly in the way he moved around the room in his white gauze pants and tunic, demonstrating poses, touching people.

At the end he said it was time to balance their chakras. He came over to Katrina last and put his hand on her abdomen. She felt a fluttering between her thighs.

"I'm getting that your second chakra is a little out of balance. Do you feel like you're always giving to everyone? You might have trouble with digestion. You might feel a little obsessive about sex?"

"Are you saying this to every woman in the room?" She smiled at him but he didn't smile back.

"You need to nurture yourself. That's what the remedy for the second chakra is. Lots of rest and relaxation. Lots of mothering."

He put his hand back to rest on her belly. She was a little self-conscious but the pressure of his palm felt good and warm. She didn't want him to move away.

When it was time to leave he was talking to three women and she just waved at him but he followed her to the door and kissed her cheek. She felt the women watching them.

"I'll see you Sunday," he said softly as the rain beat down, a sudden torrent, hard-sounding as hail. "Be careful with that second chakra. In balance it's perfect for mothering and out of balance you become a martyr."

THE BEST THINGS IN LIFE ARE WET

Katrina emailed Jasper thanking him for the workshop. At the end of the email she told him about the dream she had found in her journal; the one from November before they met.

"I am flattered but I'm not your dream man," he wrote back. "You hardly know me! Let's just get to know each other as friends."

Katrina felt her stomach sinking stonily. It was the same sensation as the regretful aftermath of a second Krispy Kreme donut, or pressing the "send" button on her computer. Why had she shared the dream? She hadn't been calling him her dream man, had she? She was anxious about going back to the dance on Sunday but Grace insisted.

"You can't leave me once," Katrina told her.

Jasper was prancing around, engaged with all sorts of women. Most of them were a lot younger than he was. He didn't touch them, though; Katrina was watching.

After class she went out into the bamboo courtyard with Grace. There was a fountain with two bronze nymphs and a sea god frolicking in the water.

Jasper came over looking especially bright-eyed.

"Have you been avoiding me?" he asked.

She started to stammer something about the dream but he

interrupted her. "Have lunch with me."

Grace squeezed her hand but she wasn't sure if it was with excitement or a warning.

"I didn't bring a change of clothes," Katrina said, plucking her sweaty T-shirt away from her chest.

"Sea, sweat, and tears. Anything can be cured with salt water."

"I have to go."

"Let me walk to your car at least."

"I'm sorry about that email," she chattered. "I mean, I wasn't calling you my dream man. I was just telling you it was weird how..."

Jasper wrapped his fingers around her upper arms and brought her toward him. When he kissed her she could hear his heart beating in his big chest. His mouth was rough and prodding and she didn't know what to do with her lips—it had been such a long time since anyone had kissed her. Her underwear was damp and a slight rain had begun to fall.

"See," he said, as she got into the car. "The best things in life."

And there was that unfamiliar sensation again. It tickled her nerve endings. It was worth anything to feel it, even for a moment. To escape. To be desired.

SWEAT

In the restaurant, giant Buddhas glowed, golden and serene, out of the darkness. They sat in a booth behind a gauzy curtain. Electronic trance music throbbed through the seats.

"Sometimes they want you to use your animal spirit name," Jasper said. "I'm Cobra Eyes. Who are you?"

He had invited her to go to a sweat lodge with him.

"I've never thought about it before. I like deer."

"You look like a deer. Your eyes. May I make a sugges-tion?"

She nodded distractedly, imagining how she might have to tell everyone at the sweat lodge that her name was Deer. Doe, a deer.

"You need to get more grounded. I see you spinning out at dance a lot. You should wear some heavier jewelry, heavy shoes. It would help."

"Why?"

She realized she must have sounded defensive because he added, "I can sometimes see what people need. Deer can be flighty, fragile."

A fire engine drove by, right on cue, sounding its alarm.

She held her leg out to show Jasper her silver ankle strap Mary Janes. "Are these hooves heavy enough?"

"These will do."

"I manifested them."

"You what?"

"I am good at manifesting shoes. I saw them in my mind and that same day I went to this cheap shoe store I never go to and they were on the front table at this ridiculously low price."

"So you can manifest shoes. What else?"

"It's best to start small and work up. Like, Grace, she wanted all these things—a house, a husband, kids. But she was afraid to try. So she picked something simple. She picked peonies because they're her favorite flower. A house full. And she was catering this wedding and it was all done in peonies and they let her take them all home. She just stuffed her house with peonies. And then later she got all her other dreams. Once she believed in it."

"So what else do you want to manifest?" Jasper asked.

She didn't want to say. She was vulnerable enough.

"How's this?"

He was kissing her. She couldn't breathe and she still wasn't sure what she was doing but it was different from the first time on the street. They were in a darkened booth with a curtain. His hands were on her thighs.

There was a phrase that kept going through her mind as their bodies struggled against each other.

"Five hundred years."

That's what she heard. Five hundred years of waiting.

But waiting for what?

The waiter came and they pulled away from each other. She was shaking. Jasper ordered for them—coconut milk curry, basmati rice, naan. She wasn't hungry at all. The Zoloft and the kiss had slain her appetite.

"I had this phrase in my head," she said. "While you were kissing me."

"What, sweetheart?"

"Five hundred years."

"What do you think it means?"

"I think I've been waiting for you."

"The woman always keeps the story," said Jasper. "The woman knows. They say a woman's prayers are thousands of times stronger than a man's."

It was pouring rain when they left the restaurant. They chewed on fennel seeds and sugar crystals on the way to the car. Jasper hoisted her in his arms so that her hips rested against his chest and her legs dangled over his arm. He bent over and slid her down onto the seat. His hand lingered on her ass for a moment and then he went around to the driver's side. She ran her hands over the taut, hard skin of his large hand drum to calm herself down.

"There's something I wanted to tell you," she said, as they drove through the falling slivers of wet sky. "I wouldn't normally bring it up but because of the sweat... I'm on this medication for depression and the package insert says there's a risk of dehydration and I thought, I've never done a sweat before."

"We have lots of special fortified water for you," he said. "And you can always leave if you don't feel okay. You can tell me and we'll leave."

They were silent for a little while. Then he added, "You don't need anti-depressants. I'll be your anti-depressant."

"You know exactly what to say, don't you?"

He smiled at her sideways. His strange blue eyes were dim with rain clouds. She held onto the drum, glad it was between them.

Kali did sweats. She told Katrina she once saw two spirits in the lodge and they were not happy. Kali said they didn't appreciate having their sacred ritual co-opted. But Katrina didn't see any spirits in the sweat lodge with Jasper. All she saw was Jasper, across from her in the darkness, next to two thin young women; they were all completely naked

Katrina hadn't planned on taking off her clothes. She'd

brought her black one-piece bathing suit and even that worried her. But everyone else was stripping, and she felt more self-conscious keeping her clothes on so she just wore a towel. After awhile she had to take it off because of the heat and she wondered how much of her body he could see. When her own myopic eyes adjusted, the other women's pale breasts seemed to swell out of the darkness. Katrina wished they weren't so close to him. One of the women kept turning her head toward Jasper as he played his drum. His voice was deep, booming through the waves of heat.

The medicine woman had them go around in a circle, stating their names. "Cobra Eyes. Mystic Deer." Stating their gratitude, stating their gifts, what they had brought to offer. Katrina felt dizzy and the sweat was in her eyes and mouth. The darkness was pressing on her temples. She wanted to touch Jasper but he was all the way on the other side of the pile of steaming rocks. The other women were close enough to touch him. Katrina couldn't tell if she was crying. She wanted air but there was only a tiny sliver of air when they opened the flap to bring in more rocks at the beginning of each round. She thought of Kali's angry spirits. And supposedly Kali had some Native American in her blood.

What would the spirits think of someone like me, dabbling in their sacred rituals, on some date with a white man who gripped their drum between his knees?

When they told each other what they were grateful for, Jasper said, "Mystic Deer."

The medicine woman asked them all to speak at the same time, revealing the things they were willing to give up.

"Fear," Katrina kept saying, over and over again. "Fear Fear Fear."

She was grateful for the Zoloft. She knew it would have been too hard for her otherwise, watching Jasper so close to the naked women.

After the sweat, she put the towel around her waist and stepped out into the rain. The cold water steamed against the warmth of her skin. Under a dripping birch tree she turned slowly with her arms raised above her head. Jasper came and took her hand. They danced like this, the mud between their toes, the rain sliding down their spines. The other women had gone inside the house. No angry spirits had followed them out of the lodge. For a moment the fear was really gone.

Jasper kissed her on the street in front her apartment, so deep and forceful it was hard for her to breathe. His fingers grazed the place between her thighs; she was wet again.

"See, you're hydrated."

"The medicine I'm on… I can't come." She said it before she could stop himself.

"We're going to fuck away all that depression. Just wait, you won't need any of that shit anymore."

She realized she was clinging to him like she was on the edge of a precipice. She loosened her grip and he pulled away, adjusting his jeans. Then he was gone into the rain like an apparition.

She spent the rest of the night in her bed, thinking of him, anorgasmic.

GRAND CROSS

Los Angeles is a scavenger hunt. Find your mind in the libraries and museums. Find your body running, hiking, biking. Find your spirit hidden in the hills, the canyons, or exposed in splendid urban squalor on the boulevards.

The next weekend Jasper took her to the Hare Krishna temple. They left their shoes on the stairs. Inside, the big, pale pink terracotta building with the lotus columns, doll-like, glass-eyed and bejeweled statues presided over an altar decked with fresh carnations. Jasper said the devotees changed the statue's costumes every day and put them into pajamas at night. The women wore brightly colored silk saris and the men had long peach robes, wooden prayer beads and shaved heads. Flowers wreathed their necks as they stood swaying to the music in front of the altar with the deities. Jasper bent down and put his forehead against the marble floor before he left. Katrina thought of doing it, too, but felt too self-conscious, then wondered if she had offended someone.

Afterwards they went to the temple's vegetarian restaurant. They ate slowly, sitting on the same side of the booth, touching the whole time. Dal and rice and salad with tahini dressing and mango halvah.

"I feel so at home here," Jasper said. "I think I was from

India in one life."

"Do you know a lot about that, past lives?"

"Some. I've had a lot of readings."

"Tell me one."

He looked at her with that hypnotic gaze and she realized she was holding her breath.

"I know I once was trying to help these women. These women who were in touch with the sacred. I was on their side but I couldn't help them. And I had to watch them being mutilated and destroyed. They were called witches and I had to watch them burn."

She gulped some air and shivered. Jasper put his arm around her shoulders.

"Have you ever been to the museum?" he asked.

It was a dark room with spot lit, disturbingly realistic wax figures that moved their hands or rolled their glass eyes while music played and a voice boomed out the history of the religion.

"Aren't they kind of creepy?" she asked him.

"Not more so than Christ on the cross. Just think if you'd never seen a crucifix," he said. "If you walked into a Catholic church for the first time."

"I guess organized religion is just a little creepy. Spirituality is so much more personal than that."

"That's why I believe in the church of myself," said Jasper, leaning over to kiss her neck. She couldn't tell if he was smiling or not. He must have been.

"Let's go," she said. The wax figures were starting to seem too real.

"There's someone I want you to meet."

It was Zephyr, a black lab waiting in the truck. Katrina stroked the dog's smooth dark head while Jasper held her in his arms.

"This is how it should be," Jasper said. "The man loves the woman and the woman gives energy to the young and the animals."

If she hadn't been on vitamin Z this would probably have made her cry. She leaned into Jasper and stroked Zephyr's chest. She could feel both their hearts beating.

When she thought of this moment, later, she understood how she let Jasper come in so far.

"I want to fuck you right now," he said.

She was still petting Zephyr. The air smelled of curry and slightly decayed carnations from the discarded garlands. Suddenly, she was afraid.

"Wait to have sex with him," Kali had said. "Wait as long as possible."

"My friend Kali did your chart."

Jasper was quiet. It was dark now; Katrina couldn't make out his eyes at all.

"What's wrong? I bet she saw my grand cross?"

"What's that?"

"It's the way the planets line up. Only saints and criminals have them, supposedly."

"Are you a criminal, Jasper?" she teased. "Tell me now."

He looked at her strangely and the smile left her face. She did see his eyes, then, by the street lamp light in front of the Hare Krishna temple. There was something otherworldly in them. "I'm not a *criminal.*" There was an emphasis on the last word that made her body cold again.

But saints never even imply they are, do they?

EX-WITCH

"What did you dream about last night?" Jasper's voice sounded soft and warm as bath water. She was lying in the tub, votives lit around her. Her body looked pretty this way, she thought, belly camouflaged with bubbles, breasts buoyed up, floating on the shimmery surface.

"I don't remember." But she didn't tell him how grateful she was not to. "What about you?"

"I've been feeling disturbed all day today. I think it was from this dream about my ex-girlfriend."

"The one that I remind you of?"

"No. Totally different woman! I don't know if I've told you about this one. I was with her before I met you."

The bath water was getting cold now but she felt suddenly paralyzed.

"It was... territorial. She was angry about something."

She waited for him to go on, trying to slide lower under the surface of the water that was still warmer than the air. Goosebumps rose on the exposed tops of her breasts. There wasn't enough water to cover them and if she added water it would be even colder. Plus, she wouldn't be able to hear his voice.

Finally she asked. "What?"

He didn't answer. He said, instead, "She is a powerful witch."

"You're powerful," she said, not missing a beat, trying not to sound freaked.

"No. Not like her. Where she is from, everyone believes that anything she says is truth, even if it hasn't happened yet. When we were together she accused me of sleeping with other women. Because she saw it—even if it was something from the past or future, but if she saw it as happening, it was true. I just stay away from her. That's the safest thing. And I never want any woman I'm seeing to have to deal with her."

I was disturbed by the story of Jasper's ex-witch. But not afraid enough to want to stay away from him, even if the woman had already seen me. Even if I were the ex-witch's disaster. Or if Jasper were mine.

ALTERED

She hadn't had an altar in the apartment.

"No wonder your life is out of balance," Kali had said.

Katrina used the top of a small built-in bookcase and covered it with a peach-colored, silver-beaded cloth, photos of her mother, of Grace and her family, candles, a vase of Stargazer lilies, a pink glass Quan Yin, the Chinese goddess of compassion, that Grace had given her. She had incense, towels, lavender soap, bottles of Canadian water, apples, almonds, and avocados. She had extra underpants and condoms.

Jasper met her at the dance place. When he saw her, he grabbed her and lifted her in the air, spun her around so the room was a carousel of dancers. He was wearing a turquoise shirt, the color of the inner ring of his irises, and as she buried her head against his chest she smelled the smoky meadow of his sweat. They danced together the whole time, oblivious to anyone else. It was the most intense foreplay she could have imagined; her dance pants were soaked through at the crotch and along with Jasper's meadow she could smell the soft musk of herself.

Finally it was all too much and Jasper lifted her, her legs around his waist and whispered, "Let's go now!" There was so much urgency in his voice that it weakened her and she had to steady herself on his arm.

He carried her over the threshold of the new house. She could feel something pressing into her side, the pendant he wore against his chest, under his shirt. The house still smelled a little of fresh paint and it was almost unnaturally quiet. A soft lemony afternoon light filtered through the panes of glass in the French doors and Katrina heard Grace's old wind chimes tinkling. Katrina was glad Grace had left them behind; it felt almost as if she were there.

He lay Katrina on the floor and sprawled out beside her. He looked twice her length. When he leaned over her, she saw what was around his neck — a cord with a small pouch attached to it.

"What's that?" she asked, fingering the soft red leather.

"My talisman. There's something in it for you, too."

He took it off and slid an object out of the pouch. It was a silver ring.

"A friend of mine gave this to me a few years ago," he said. "It belonged to his ex-girlfriend. He said I should give it to the woman who is the one."

The one? A chill went along her spine. The one the one the one. She thought of Daniel. He had been her one; she knew she was never his.

But who was this ex-girlfriend? Wasn't that a bad omen, too? Still, she was someone's one. He had carried her over her threshold and given her a ring.

"Spread your legs," he murmured. She lay on the floor and watched him undress. The wood felt hard against her lower back.

"I used to always want tall, skinny women," Jasper said. "Except for Esther — the one like you. You're both so little and soft."

He didn't enter her; his penis wasn't hard.

"I haven't been able to get hard enough since my last girlfriend. I think she put a hex on me."

Katrina wanted to believe he was protecting her from the wrath of his ex-witch. It would have been a better explanation for her ego. It would have been romantic, noble, kept the illusion that she was appreciated intact. She wanted to believe Jasper's penis was hexed. It was less hurtful than realizing he just couldn't get hard for her

He reached inside with his fingers and then what felt like his whole hand. She undulated and bucked around like she was giving birth. He knew exactly what to do and she was pouring wet but she didn't come.

They were on the wooden floor beneath the altar. Along with the incense, flowers, fruits and candles, she knew she was an offering.

Kali saw the bruises all over Katrina's body when she was doing a headstand in yoga the next day. Kali's eyes flashed until Katrina grinned at her lasciviously and winked.

"So much for waiting," Kali said.

Something wasn't right about it; Katrina knew. She was purple and yellow. She was small and soft. A toy. But carried over the threshold. Ringed.

DREAM WEDDING
December 5, 1998

It rained the night before so the air literally twinkles. The statues of saints, angels, and deities from every culture that stand hidden among the foliage have been anointed, awash in light. Saint Francis, Mary, Buddha, Krishna, Quan Yin, Tara. The creek bed that runs alongside the patio is full and the sound of rushing water floats beneath the music.

The day is more like a dream. More vivid and real than life, the way dreams can sometimes be.

Grace and Gerald chose the Inn of the Seventh Ray in Topanga for their wedding because it was where they had gone for brunch on their first date and they thought it was one of the most beautiful places in the city. Grace said she thought Topanga Canyon was like the city's heart. Still wild and mysterious, uncorrupted.

She'd asked me to do the flowers and I'd never done that before but it was easier than I'd thought. I went to the Mart downtown at dawn the day before to purchase the pale pink peonies and roses for the tables. I put petals into the fountain and tied Grace's bouquet in yards of cream tulle.

Grace agreed to let me wear black, even though I knew she really wanted the bridesmaids in white. Her own dress is an antique cream satin gown. She has a wreath of tea roses in her hair instead of a veil.

When I see her walking down the stairs into the patio I try to blink away tears to keep my makeup from running but it doesn't help; I'm streaked. She really does look angelic. I see Gerald flick at his eyes, too. He seems so large and solid, bigger than anyone in the garden, waiting for her.

After the ceremony, we eat salmon and salad and cake. The strings of fairy lights twink on when the sun goes down and we dance late into the night. Daniel holds me and whispers, "Maybe we should see if they're booked for next June," but he's drunk on too much white wine and champagne.

Later, at home, when Daniel and I are making love I can't help thinking about Gerald carrying Grace over the threshold. How she must have looked to him placing the wreath of now-crushed roses on his big head and laughing. Making him close his eyes while she let her dress fall to the floor. "Now all I'm wearing is the only thing I'm never going to take off." How he must have held her as if she were the most precious person in the whole world.

SCARRED

Jasper had a huge scar that ran down the side of his leg and across his pelvis. He told Katrina that when he was seventeen he almost died in a motorcycle accident. She liked to feel the rough ridges where he was sewn back together, imagine how he could have been taken away forever.

Every scar has a story; some have myths.

This was Jasper's: When he was little his parents divorced and his mother took him and his sister to California. They lived in a gingerbread house in the Haight, went to love-ins and outdoor concerts in Golden Gate Park. Then one day Jasper's father and his new wife came to take the children for a vacation and never brought them back. Jasper was beaten regularly. He wrote to his mother begging her to come rescue him but she never did.

"I had no inner mother," Jasper said. "That's why I got in that accident."

But he liked to look at the positive side of things; while he was recovering in the hospital, he began to meditate, to write in a journal, to draw, to become an artist. "A spiritual being," he said.

"And when I got out," Jasper added, "I met my girlfriend. She was a beautiful model."

What other kind is there? Katrina wondered. Her skin had started to itch.

"But I left her," Jasper said. "Before she could leave me. I worshipped her. It's different with you," he added. "You're real."

Enlightened American women aren't supposed to admit that they are scarred by the fact that they don't look like supermodels. It wasn't spiritually correct, as Kali would have said. Of course, she *did* look like one. Jasper's scars were huge, dramatic, implying death. Katrina's were invisible, private, even shameful.

After Jasper's accident, his mother was diagnosed with schizophrenia.

"She thought I was the devil," he told Katrina. "She put crosses up all over the house and warned me to stay away."

This in itself was another warning, of course, but her own scars kept her from listening. She was busy imagining ways to disguise the damage.

MOVING IS GOOD

She moved into her new house on a weekend. Grace had helped her pack methodically by room, marking the boxes with a Sharpie, throwing away as much as she took. Kali said she'd help her feng shui the house. She told Katrina, "All your possessions should be either beautiful or useful; things sense when you don't like them and that creates more negativity."

Lise's artwork, mismatched floral thrift shop china, baking utensils, glass vases from flowers boyfriends had sent over the years, tea lights, candleholders, art supplies, CDs, and books. Books on myth and fairy tales and poetry and children's picture books, including the fragile, yellowing ones from her childhood. *Alice in Wonderland; Peter Pan; The Lion, the Witch and the Wardrobe; The Hobbit* — books she wanted to live inside. She had more room for her clothes in the new house but she threw away the things that were too small, that she'd been saving with the hopes of fitting into one day; they made her too depressed. So the closet had her mostly black and sometimes lacy thrift shop dresses, her chunky-heeled, round-toed, ankle-strapped shoes and splurged-on handbags, the soft, silver-flecked scarves and sweaters she knitted, her strings of bright beads and charm bracelets that the children loved to finger when they wept in her arms as their parents left for the day.

The unpacking made Katrina feel like she did when she was a child playing with her dollhouse. Her mother had made the house; in fact, she had once done an entire art exhibit of miniature houses with mysterious scenes played out inside. One had a doll drowning in the bathtub, another showed a priest in his chapel, looking into a crystal ball, still another had rows of birdcages on the roof—they were filled with tiny girls with gauze wings. The one she made for Katrina was a Victorian painted like Neapolitan ice cream with a real fountain full of tiny mermaids. Katrina and her mother put up the lace curtains, placed the birthday candles in the silver chandelier, hung the tiny mirror behind the washbasin, arranged the blue and white china plates and the silverware that was small enough to fit on a thumbnail.

Now, unpacking in Grace's old house, Katrina felt that sense of home again. She wished she could say the same about being in her body. When she moved it in the dance she forgot the extra weight, lost self-consciousness. But when she stopped dancing, even for a moment, even in her prettiest black silk and lace and tulle thrift shop dress with the silver rhinestone buttons, she was naked with Jasper. His.

FLOWERS SMELL BETTER THAN OLD DOGS

As a housewarming present to herself, she bought flowers. That's what she told herself, pretending it had nothing to do with seduction. Stargazer lilies, lysantheum, freesia, white roses. The front room smelled so sweet, intoxicating. She re-arranged her altar with some sari fabric and two tiny painted goddesses that Kali had brought her—Laksmi and Saraswati, abundance and good fortune. Lots of candles. Fixing up the house made Katrina less obsessive about Jasper, less worried when she didn't hear from him for a couple of days.

Jasper called late that night. He said he was at a party nearby and asked if he could come over. She knew she was supposed to say it was too late, she was already busy or something but of course she just told him he could come.

She lit the candles and sat on the floor with all the flowers around her. Finally, when he still didn't come, she sat on the couch with the dogs, watching some bad television drama.

It was a lot later when he finally arrived, more dressed up than she had ever seen him in an embroidered silk shirt. The dogs nuzzled together, trying to put their heads in his lap. He patted them absently, his mouth twisted slightly with distaste.

"Zephyr gets a bath with tea tree oil every two weeks. It really helps."

"Sorry for the smell," she said. "I wash them, too. They're kind of old guys."

"It's really strong when you first walk in."

"Sorry."

He got up and walked to the case with the collection of children's books.

"What are these?"

"I just love them. Plus, you know I teach. And I love kids."

"So why don't you have any?" He was staring at her fiercely now. She felt her face color.

"I lost one. Never got to use these child-baring hips."

"Well, it's probably for the best. They say it's usually because there is something wrong."

The dogs came over and competed to put their noses into her palm. As if they sensed she needed them.

"You wouldn't say that if you'd been through it," Katrina said. "It doesn't feel like 'for the best.' It feels like hell."

"I have been through it," Jasper said. "Twice. Different girlfriends. Although one may have been cheating on me so I can't say for sure if it was mine to begin with."

Katrina wondered if she should go to him, try to comfort him somehow; she just sat there.

"It was for the best," he said.

She could manifest shoes but she hadn't been able to manifest a husband, a real baby. Slim hips. Or a guarantee that she wouldn't dream of the apocalypse.

Had she manifested Jasper?

Then he came and put his arm around her. She stroked the sueded silk of his shirt.

"It was a clothing optional party," Jasper said. "Tonight. Tantra group. I remember how shy you were at the sweat. I didn't think you'd be comfortable."

She felt her skin go cold, as if she were naked now.

Jasper took her hands. She wanted to pull away. "I hope I

didn't upset you talking about the babies? It's just easier to look at it that way."

"I never got over it, I guess," she said.

"I know. Let's try something, okay? Sit with me and look into my eyes."

She noticed for the first time that his left eye looked much smaller than his right. The room started to spin and she was wet between her thighs, her skin flushed, she forgot that she'd been cold.

Jasper took off his clothes and lay down. Katrina cuddled into his armpit. He didn't touch her.

"Just close your eyes," Jasper said. "You will dream of only sweet things. When you wake up you are going to be all fresh like a little flower. Loving your body. Loving everything. All the trauma will be gone. I want you to taper your meds starting tomorrow."

She still hadn't told him about her nightmares. He just knew. Maybe he was going to be her shaman. He was going to rescue her from the disaster of herself.

FOR THE BEST
November 1, 1999

A thicket of red roses. I keep tearing my hands on the thorns as I try to rip through them. Blood pours down my wrists.

Under the roses is a glass box. Inside it a little girl is sleeping. Long brown hair, pale skin. She looks like a princess in a white dress.

When I woke up next to Daniel there was blood all over my underwear.

She was only a blinking dot on an ultrasound screen but that was her heart! I wrote to her every night in my journal. I already loved her.

I didn't even wake Daniel; I took the phone into the bathroom and called Grace. My baby was gone.

PAST LIVES

Kali wanted to do a ritual to bless the house. The women sat in a circle in their white dresses; she put bindis on their foreheads and smudged the rooms with sage.

"Grace is the Mother," Kali said. "I'll be the Crone. Katrina, you're the Maiden."

"The maiden aunt," Katrina said.

"It's not looking that way. When am I going to meet him?"

Katrina didn't want to admit that she was afraid to introduce Kali to Jasper.

"Soon."

"Katrina," she said. "I think you and I have some healing to do. It goes back a long, long way. Lifetimes."

Kali turned to face her and took her hands. Katrina couldn't look into Kali's eyes. She felt tears coming up fast and furiously hot, tried to squeeze them back which made them fatter. She wondered what Kali knew about their past life. Had one stolen the other's love? Betrayed the other? Had one been dragged by the hair up on a platform and burned at the stake?

Kali said, "There was a woman I worked with once. She had breast cancer, lost her job, her husband left her. While we were doing the regression, she said she saw a man, some kind of vampireish figure, very hot looking in a long dark coat. And he was killing this woman, basically fucking her to death, the woman said. Blood was everywhere. And somewhere in the middle of that the woman changed the pronoun from 'he' to 'I.' But she didn't realize she'd done it and when I told her she started freaking out, all of a sudden she got that she was the man! That her suffering was her soul punishing her for what she had done in the past. When she became conscious and found forgiveness, her life started to heal.

"So we don't know if we were the victim or the perpetrator. It's harder to accept being the perp. But it's a cycle that keeps repeating until we get conscious."

Katrina still couldn't look into Kali's eyes. Her face felt blister-hot.

"I'm sorry, Kali,"

"I'm sorry, too. We're just too much alike."

Katrina knew they weren't really the same at all. Kali had danced with a snake around her shoulders. It had looked into her eyes and she was no longer afraid of a man fucking around on her or rejecting or abandoning her. Katrina was still ruled by those fears.

Kali said, "We call on the Maiden in Her Beauty and Her Tenderness. We call on the Mother in Her Love and Her Nurturing. We call on the Crone in her Infinite Wisdom. All three live within each of us."

After the ritual they went into the garden and danced for each other. Then Gerald brought Sarah and Benji, and they ate the vegetarian potluck. Kali sat next to Katrina on the grass, slowly chewing her couscous. She wore a long white lace dress and her hair was up on her head, a bun held with chopsticks, hibiscus flowers tucked in.

"Are you doing okay?" she asked.

"You helped me," Katrina said. She realized, even as she said it, that her voice sounded pleading, rather than grateful. "You called him in. Remember our session when I asked for help?"

Kali smiled wickedly. "We're getting terribly good at manifesting, aren't we?"

"I'm going to have a party," Katrina announced. "It's his birthday. You'll meet him then."

She tried to catch Grace's eye but Grace was sitting alone, staring across off across the shadowy lawn.

NOT A PRETTY WORD
December 13, 1999

Grace and Gerald sat me down today and said, "We have something to tell you." Those are never good words.

"My cancer came back," Grace said.

"What? Your what?"

"I had it before. When I was twenty. They thought they got it all."

"What kind?"

"Melanoma. I hate that word. Mel-a-nom-a. Couldn't they call it something else?"

"Skin cancer, right? That's not that serious, is it? I mean, they just remove the…"

"It's pretty serious but it's going to be okay. I've fought it once already."
Her voice changed, then, got weaker. I could see she was remembering. I hadn't known anything about this. Why hadn't she told me?

I held her and she buried her face in my hair. I remembered my mom saying they'd found a lump in her breast. When she told me I got up and ran out the front door of our house into the canyon. I ran as fast as I could down the winding hill. Cars whizzed past, dangerously close. No sidewalk. Some guys shouted at me, "Big ass!" I turned to glare at them, my face red and bloated with tears. "Oooh ugly!" they yelled.

Gerald put his arm around both our shoulders

"Don't worry, guys. I'm going to kick this motherfucker cancer's ass," Grace said.

HOW TO GIVE TOO MUCH

It was his birthday but Katrina called the party a house-warming, so it wouldn't seem as if she were being too generous. Of course, she knew she was being too generous.

But then Jasper would say just the right thing and make her forget.

While she was running around getting everything ready, he stood up from the bed where he'd been reclining, put his arms around her waist and held her still.

"Let's not forget each other," he said. "If we're feeling disconnected, let's stop and check in. It's more important that we're doing okay together than that we try to give to everyone else."

She hugged him. At moments like that it seemed all right to offer everything you had—cake, bed, kisses, sex. It seemed appropriate and natural.

There were very few people she knew at the party. Of course, Grace and Gerald, who brought a purple *phalaenopsis* orchid and a bottle of aqua green crystalline orchid food, but mostly it was Jasper's friends, and they were mostly female. Katrina recognized a few from dance and his yoga workshop. She watched Jasper entertaining so many lovely women but she was okay with it until Kali swept in.

Katrina's heart was Jasper's drum and her hands were shaking. She realized then that she'd gone off the Zoloft way too fast. Why hadn't she tapered more slowly? Why had she taken his advice about stopping it all?

"I want you to come with me and cry with me," he had said. "I will drink your tears."

So there he was, salivating over Kali, his eyes completely blind to anyone else, his whole body alerted to her like an animal with its prey. Katrina could actually feel herself dissolving, blood boiling her down to nothing but bone. Jealousy might be a key to spells of invisibility, she thought.

Jasper had told her that he'd rather hear what she was feeling than have her hide it from him, hadn't he? She took his hand and led him into the bedroom.

"What's wrong?" he asked. "Are you scared?"

She nodded, suddenly mute.

"Are you upset that I'm talking to so many women?"

Just then Grace came in. She was eyeing Jasper suspiciously.

"Are you okay?" she asked.

Katrina nodded again.

"You don't look it." Then she added quickly, "I mean, you're always beautiful…" Grace stared deep into Katrina's eyes and cocked her head slightly to the side, in that concerned way she had. "We have to leave now. I'm calling you in the morning and we're going to talk about this."

She kissed Katrina and whispered, "I'm worried, mamacita."

"It's okay."

Katrina watched Gerald wrap a piece of silk around Grace's fragile shoulders before they went out the door. Jasper took Katrina's hand and led her into the living room. She was glad Grace had interrupted them and that she hadn't told Jasper about Kali. It didn't really matter; he was still her boyfriend, he hadn't done anything wrong. Maybe she could forget the whole thing.

"Can I use these?"

He was holding one of her three pink wine glasses between his thumb and first finger. The fourth one had shattered during the move. Katrina had bought plastic for the party.

"It just doesn't taste the same," he said to Kali, filling the glass.

She thanked him and walked away. Katrina brought out the chocolate cake she'd made and held it while he blew the candles out.

After everyone left, they danced together. Because of the way the candles framed the large front windows it felt to Katrina as if they were on stage, part of a play.

"Come to bed, baby," he said, and she forgot that she'd been upset at all.

But he brought it up again while she lay in his arms. "Are you still mad about all those women?"

"It wasn't about all those women," she said, stiffening.

"What was it about?"

"I was scared to introduce you to Kali. I was afraid you'd be really attracted to her."

Jasper's voice was calm; just the same as always, except maybe even more of a monotone. "I am attracted to her," he said. "She's very attractive. She has a powerful sexual and romantic energy about her. But you're the one I'm connecting with."

Why did she react so strongly? It felt like she'd been gassed, annihilated, instead of just mildly insulted.

When she was little, she'd been obsessed with Anne Frank. Maybe every poetic, sensitive, dark-eyed, thirteen-year-old girl does after reading that diary. But her mother got her a diary for her birthday, a little brown leather volume with a gold lock and key and Katrina named it Kitty, too and signed her entries, Anne. She drew Anne's face again and again, those huge dark, sort of mischievous eyes and that sad smile. She always kept a diary after that, and she always thought of Kitty when she wrote in it.

"What's wrong?" Jasper asked.

"I didn't ask you if you were attracted to her. I said I was afraid you would be. I don't want to hear everything you are thinking."

"But that's part of a loving relationship. We should be able to share it all."

She started coughing, then; the kind of cough that feels as if it will turn you inside out. Jasper put his hand on her back.

"You're upset, baby. That's okay. It's good to get rid of it."

Here, man, have my chocolate cake, have my girlfriends (dressed up in beaded velvet, singing you Happy Birthday), have my bed, have my sex. While you're at it, I'll give you my soul again. It has been waiting for you for five hundred years.

THE THREE GRACES

In the morning things were different; they took a walk with the dogs through the park. The grass was agleam with dew and the air was quiet and fresh. Zephyr ran ahead, without a leash; Jasper didn't believe in them. Katrina asked if he was worried about the cars.

"No. Z knows. One time I was across the street from him and he was running to me and this car nicked his leg. I didn't have time to call out for him to stop. It was the best way he could have learned."

Jasper had learned from his motorcycle accident, too, but she wasn't convinced that it was any way to teach. She didn't say that, though. Zephyr looked happier than Bilbo and Frodo, who strained on their leashes while he ran gracefully ahead, a slight limp in his back leg.

Jasper followed Katrina into the house, pushed his pelvis up against her hips, lifted her hair and kissed her neck. Then he slid his hand down inside the drawstring waistband of her sweatpants. She climbed up onto the couch and thrust her ass in the air. Jasper yanked her pants off. He slid his fingers along her wetness till he found the opening and dove inside with his hand.

She was so gone, in so much pleasure, that she hardly heard

his voice.

"I'm glad you like my hand, baby. My last girlfriend, she didn't like my hand. I told her, but my hand is more intimate than my penis. It's how I can express my love for you."

Could it be that he was actually talking about his ex-girlfriend? Was she a model? Katrina didn't give a fuck at the moment. She was coming. Multiple times to make up for all that anorgasmia.

"Tell me you need me," Jasper whispered urgently, into her ear.

"I need you."

"Tell me like you mean it."

"I need you," she moaned. "I need you so much." The phone was ringing but she hardly heard it. She had forgotten that Grace had promised to call.

They bought organic fruit and eggs and maple syrup, tea lights and lavender body oil. Jasper made pancakes and Katrina blended mango smoothies. He played the CDs he'd brought and she lit more candles. He fucked her with his hand.

"You never get sore," he said. "You're amazing. You're as into sex as I am. The women I meet are never as into sex as I am."

He touched himself on the bed while she danced for him, stripping off her clothes, undulating, crouching on hands and knees with her rear end in his face.

"Show me your breasts. Show me your yoni. Spread your legs. I can smell you."

His commands made her hotter. By saying the parts of her body out loud, he was making them real. It was as if all those pieces of her hadn't existed since the last time a man had touched her.

When they got to the dance place, later that day, Jasper said, "How do you feel about me dancing with other women?"

Something about the way he asked made her feel wary. She

asked why.

"I don't want you to get bored with me. My last girlfriend, she left me for my best friend. She got bored. I wasn't entertaining enough. I feel like you'll get tired of only dancing with me."

"I love to dance with you."

"It's so good for me how naturally monogamous you are," said Jasper, squeezing her. "If you feel you're hitting your red line, let me know. I'll stop, okay? Like a safe word. Let me know."

Once they got inside he put his arms around her and she immediately forgot her fear. After awhile she was even able to dance away from him and find Grace.

"Are you okay? I tried to call."

"We had a fight but then today was good," Katrina said.

"Are you sure?"

"Grace, I feel alive. I mean, fuck, I've felt like a dead person for years."

Later, Katrina was at the altar and Jasper was next to her and there was another woman, the woman who had held his hand in the circle on the day they met. Her skin was a warm goldish color, her eyes were bright green, cat eyes. Short hair, pierced nose, no bra, gold goddess sandals. And this: Jasper was holding her hand. He reached out and took Katrina's hand, too. For a moment they were the three Graces, swaying together like figures on a Grecian frieze. *Aren't we lovely in a classical way?* Even Jasper had a feminine flow to his long body.

Katrina untangled her fingers from his and danced away. She wasn't going to get angry. *Pretend you are still on Vitamin Z. He's just holding her hand, so what?*

After awhile Jasper let go of her and followed Katrina to the other side of the room where they danced together. Everything was going to be fine, she told herself. She wanted Grace to hold her but Grace was gone.

Jasper was quiet and solemn on the way home. She asked

him what was wrong.

"You scared me when we were making love before."

"What? I scared you?"

"You sounded so needy."

"You told me to say I needed you."

"Yes, but you said it so convincingly."

By the time they got home it was starting to rain. Jasper brought out a piece of leftover chocolate cake from the night before. Two forks.

"Are you okay?" he asked her.

She shrugged. He asked if he could prepare a bath for them before he had to leave.

"The best things in life are wet," he said with a smile that looked as if a puppeteer had pulled strings on the sides of his mouth.

He lit candles, put in gardenia oil and brought their plates of cake. Nothing really helped. Katrina sat crunched against the side of the tub, away from Jasper, hiding her stomach, trying to figure out what was going on.

"You seem depressed," he said.

"I just feel sad that the weekend is over."

"It's the unspoken things that can ruin a relationship." He paused. "Do you want me to wash you?"

She drew away. Didn't want his touch for once.

"I think it can be the spoken things."

"I disagree. I think honesty is best. At dance, I felt I was just realizing there wasn't going to be that first thrill anymore. The feelings of excitement when you first meet someone. The chase."

"The chase!" She pushed her body back, harder against the porcelain. She could feel the bruises that had never gone away, that kept getting more tender from having sex on the wooden floor even though they now had a bed in the house.

"I need to tell you what's really going on with me so you don't pick it up unconsciously. It's better to deal with things head on."

    She got out of the bath and wrapped herself in a towel. Then she told him to leave and he did.

NOT BREATHING

Kali's early morning yoga class the next day. When Katrina sat up from her child's pose she saw someone behind her, reflected in the mirror. She saw the red birthmark like a livid valentine.

"You have to breathe," Kali whispered. "This is yoga, remember? Not deep sea diving."

During corpse pose she massaged Katrina's temples and feet. Kali's hands were big and masculine, more like a man's. Katrina squeezed out quiet tears. She could feel Kali's black feather ponytail brush against her bare arms. No wonder Jasper had announced his attraction to her, Katrina thought. She couldn't blame him for that. In fact, maybe the reason she had reacted so strongly was that she wanted Kali to herself.

She ran outside after class. It had started to rain again. Jasper followed her, still barefoot. He stood on the pavement with the raindrops catching in his hair. He grabbed her arm and she tried to pull away.

"I need to talk to you."

"Why did you come here? You needed a hit of her romantic and sexual energy?"

"I wanted to see you. Please let's talk."

She started to walk away and he ran after, through the rain, in his bare feet.

"The woman I was dancing with... I met her the day I met you."

"What are you talking about?" She could feel her whole throat closing up.

"I didn't see her again until yesterday. It triggered all kinds of feelings for me. I was powerfully attracted to her but she didn't come to my workshop. You did."

The adrenaline was pumping so hard through her body that she could hardly keep from slamming her fist into his stomach or running away down the rainy street. Why hadn't she tapered the Zoloft? She imagined her nerves like a mass of raw ground beef.

"I don't want to hear your process, Jasper. Can you please just keep it to yourself?"

"That wouldn't be fair. To either of us. I need to tell my truth. My truth is that I felt you giving so much generous love this weekend. And it scared me. I'm not used to it. It triggered my fears of commitment. I didn't know how to integrate it. And then she turned up. If I had told you about my feelings for her right away, yesterday, you might not have felt so depressed."

"No, you're right. I wouldn't have been depressed. I would have been fucking pissed off angry like I am now. I don't care if you were attracted to someone else. Just don't share it with me. Don't share all your shit with me all the time."

"That's not how I choose to be in relationship," Jasper said. "I choose to communicate freely and honestly with my partner."

He turned and walked slowly away, so calmly, as if enclosed in a bubble, as if the rain was not even touching his body.

That day at school she felt the hot shivers of a flu, the tingly ache in her scalp, and she went home and crawled into bed. Grace came over with miso soup and Emergen-C vitamin packets and climbed under the covers next to her.

"I don't want you to catch it," Katrina said.

"Love makes you immune. I figured that out after I had my kids. I have my hands in their snot all day and I never catch their colds." She looked around the room. Sunlight made lacy patterns on the walls and they could hear the windchimes tinking outside.

"I love this room. It's where Gerald and I made them."

"I know," Katrina said. "I think about it all the time. I tried to explain it to Jasper once but he didn't seem to hear me..."

"Why are you still with him, mamacita?" Grace asked. Her hands felt cool on Katrina's temples.

"I can't seem to stop," Katrina said.

DREAM THEORY

I am crouching on the ground, shoving handfuls of my dog's shit into my mouth. Toxic, shocked, unable to stop.

Jasper says, "According to Jungian dream theory all the parts of our dream are really parts of us."

I wanted to explain that I'd read Jung but I couldn't talk because of what was in my mouth, making me gag.

"So what part of you do you think is shit?" he asks me.

VALENTINE

On Valentine's, sun slanted in through the bay windows of Neverland. The children were gathered in a circle listening to some of the parents play chamber music. The air smelled buttery-sweet from the heart cookies the children had baked earlier that morning. Benji and Sarah were sitting on Katrina's lap, their curls smelling like baby shampoo, their fingers curled around her own, but Katrina was thinking about Jasper. If he would bring her roses and chocolate. If they would have sex. Even after everything that had happened.

Why do we have to be terminal or in love to appreciate life properly?

THE CLIFF

They were going to go find a waterfall.

Instead they found a cliff.

She drove to his house that morning. He'd never invited her before, always making some kind of excuse.

Jasper's house was actually his mother's. He told Katrina that he had to move in with her when she wasn't able to manage by herself. In spite of the fact that she had called him the devil, he told Katrina he felt obligated to do what he could.

On her way up La Brea she saw a cluster of plaster statues in a mini-mall parking lot. Michelangelo's *David* and Botticelli's *Venus* looked suspiciously like porn stars in the harsh, smoggy morning light, but there was also a huge, sloe-eyed Quan Yin surrounded by rabbits. Katrina swerved into the lot and bought her, even though her hand was chipped. She knew she needed a big goddess as she drove up into the hills under the Hollywood sign. She thought of how it used to say "Hollywoodland" and then imagined "Quakeland" written out jaggedly across the landscape.

The house was an old red brick building with a green roof. It had a darkly overgrown garden; Jasper told her he had wanted to landscape it for his mother but she wouldn't let him; she felt safer with the thick tangle of foliage protecting her from the world, he said. Katrina's blood surged with anxiety when she knocked at the door, like a child in a fairytale who knows she should turn back but, somehow, can't.

Jasper answered wearing a flannel shirt, jeans, and hiking boots. The sight of him—long-legged, five o'clock shadowed, rugged—reassured her for a moment. She peered past him into the dim rooms. What she saw was an odd mix of new age and old. Candles and incense burned on an altar and she glimpsed Jasper's drum. But there was also some overstuffed furniture and bad oil paintings in ugly gold frames.

Scratchy mumblings from another room. Jasper rolled his eyes.

"Mother's had a hard morning," he said. "She doesn't want me going out."

Mother? Who called their parent that? Maybe Anthony Perkins in *Psycho*.

"She told me she put a curse on me today," Jasper said, rolling his eyes.

Because of the recent rains, the roads that led to the waterfall trail were closed. Jasper asked some bikers in a local gas station where another scenic spot might be. One big guy with tattoos and a goatee told him where the hike began.

The sun was bright and hot in a faintly blue, washed-out sky. The landscape reminded Katrina of some dreams she'd had of pale sand, jagged rock, sparse dead-looking trees. They took a path that wound above a sand bed where water trickled. Many rock piles blocked their way. Jasper said the rocks must have fallen recently during the rains. She shivered, imagining a landslide so close to where they lay. She wondered why she was there at all.

Every so often, Jasper would stop and grab her, stick his tongue in her mouth and grab her ass. She felt dizzy in the bright light. And from the blood making its way out of her; it was the second day of her period.

They got to the top of a cliff. Below them sparse trees lined a riverbed. Dark water snaked along. Birds shrieked.

Jasper wanted to eat the picnic he'd told her to bring so they sat at the side of the trail on the edge of that cliff. It felt terribly exposed—to the hard, white sky, the loose rock piles, any hikers who chanced to walk by. But Katrina was already feeling the sex spell slowing her limbs. She just did what he said.

They started on the cashew butter and jam sandwiches she'd made and then Jasper tossed his aside with an expression of distaste.

"There's something I've been wanting to tell you."

She braced but the spell was still strong enough that she didn't pull away from him.

"It's about your kisses. I don't want to feel your teeth. Could you be more careful?"

She put a hand to her mouth. "Oh my God, I'm so sorry. Why didn't you say something? I'm so embarrassed." She wasn't aware that she'd done that at all. If anything, it felt like Jasper was forcing his mouth on hers most of the time.

"It's all right. I just like my tongue. I want to keep it in tact."

Her stomach did a slow flip. It really felt like the whole thing just turned over; could it be? No one had ever criticized her kissing before. Jasper started massaging her thighs through her blue jeans. She was swollen with blood so the seam at her crotch pushed into her, swelling her more. Her pelvis had a life of its own, working against Jasper's hand. He unzipped her jeans and slid them half way off, then lay her out on the small picnic blanket. She could feel sharp rocks under her butt, bits of gravel embedding into her. Kali had told her the new hipster trend was to embed metal pieces under the skin to make designs, instead of tattoos, another way to decorate the body. Maybe the gravel would show up in patterns—constellations and flowers.

She knew she was lying there, bleeding, exposed to man

and nature, jeans halfway down, butt ground into sharp rocks, but she didn't struggle, she didn't try to move. She heard the papery, crunching sound of her menstrual pad as Jasper shoved his hand between her legs. His fingers went up inside of her, finding the spot against the wall of her womb that made her fall apart, made her his. His whole hand seemed to be inside of her. She felt out of control, at his mercy, like some kind of puppet.

These are the words Jasper said to Katrina while he was fucking her with his hand on a cliff:

"I'm so glad I found you. There are other women who are more attractive to me, thinner or whatever, but it's better this way. It's not too much of a distraction."

She felt it like a punch to her gut. Her whole body convulsed around itself and she slithered away from him, backwards, reptilian almost, trying to pull on her jeans and adjust the bloody pad. Blood was on Jasper's hand, too, and she could smell it. The sun flared off the water in the riverbed and she was blinded for a moment.

"What are you saying?" she shrieked. Her voice sounded like the birds they had heard earlier, circling above, birds of prey. She put her arms around her torso and rocked back and forth, squeezing the flesh at her sides with her thumb and forefinger. When he reached out to touch her with his bloody hand, she skittered away again.

"I'm so sorry," said Jasper. He had a stunned look on his face.

"How could you say that to me?"

"I just meant that I love you. The way you look isn't even important. It's who you are."

"Never say that to me again."

"I won't, baby. I'm sorry."

Then all the tears that the Zoloft had claimed came out of her. When she looked up, Jasper had tears in his eyes, too.

This made her stop for a moment.

"It's just that when I don't see my own beauty, I can't see yours. I have to be able to see my beauty so that I can love you. Please forgive me."

He put his arms around her and she let him. Too weak to fight. She wanted to get off the cliff, back to the car, home. She realized there was no way to escape without his help.

On the hike back down, they came to a huge pile of rocks blocking the path. As they climbed over them, Jasper tried to take her hand but she waved him away.

"These weren't here before," he said. "It must have happened just now."

This gave her a chill—imagining a landslide so close to where they lay. The sun was starting to set, too, and the air had a bite. Jasper babbled on as they walked.

"My next-to-last girlfriend, did I tell you about her? The one who didn't like my hand? I went hiking with her once, and I told her, 'I love you so much I want to just push you off the side of a cliff.' Have you ever loved someone that much? She left me for my best friend. She got bored with me. That was why I was worried that you would get bored with me. Anyway, she was only seventeen. Did I tell you that?"

"Why are you telling me, Jasper?"

"I was trying to figure out why I said those things. Why I was so mean. Maybe I was scared you would leave me. I wasn't seeing my beauty."

"Maybe she didn't leave you because she was bored with you," Katrina said. "Maybe you hurt her."

Jasper was sauntering down the trail, a tall, graceful figure. The dead trees and the snake river below. The sky darkening. The air cooling to goosebump temperature. The rocks threatening to slide. "No. Actually, with her, I just worshipped her. I worshipped her too much. I treated her like a goddess and she couldn't deal with it. It was too much for her."

She tried to count her breaths—one in, one out, two in, two

out, three in, three out, up to ten, start again. *Don't speak don't speak don't speak*. But in the car, on the freeway headed for home, he asked why she was still quiet, if she was still angry.

"So, with her, with your seventeen-year-old girlfriend, you worshipped her too much. That was the problem."

Jasper nodded.

"And with me, you just get mean."

"With you and Esther, the one who you reminded me of. It's because I wasn't in touch with my own beauty."

Katrina turned away and pressed her hot forehead against the chilly glass. Why couldn't she stop asking? "But you were in touch with your beauty around the seventeen-year-old."

"She was seventeen!" Jasper said. "She was a model, like my first girlfriend!"

"What is that supposed to mean?" This time she screamed it. "That I'm too old and fat for you? What if I told you that your penis wasn't big or hard enough?"

She really felt like she was going to throw up, like she had to get out of the car right away. She gripped the door handle and kept her head against the glass, trying to remain very still. Jasper was talking, on and on. She tried to stop listening, counting her breath. Then she heard him say, "You know what the problem is? You're not in touch with your shadow self."

She rolled her eyes but didn't answer him. Tried to breathe away the building nausea. Blood was cramping in her pelvis.

"It's the dark side we don't acknowledge. You need to face your shadow better and work with it so it doesn't come out in these angry zingers all the time. Did you hear your voice just now? You've got some biggies there. It might help to do some shadow work. If you have that kind of self-hatred, especially about a part of your body, it can manifest as disease."

She turned to watch him chattering as he drove. His eyes looked pale in the darkness. She didn't tell him how well she knew her shadow. She didn't want him to have it.

"Oh shit!" he said.

"What?"

"There's blood on my shirt. From you."

ABANDONMENT ISSUES

She knew she should have broken up with Jasper that day on the cliff but she couldn't do it. And she couldn't tell Grace what happened. Too ashamed. Kali was different, though.

"The only way you can feel validated as a woman is through a man," Kali said. "And the more potentially painful the man is to you the more valuable his attention is because if he likes you instead of his beautiful seventeen-year-old model, then you really are a woman?"

Miss Mousey had a spousey...

It was like asphyxiation. She couldn't get any words out except, "I don't want to be alone. My dad..."

The truth was, she couldn't even remember her father. All she knew was that he was some kind of guru with a following of women. Her mother had just been another acolyte.

"That feeling of abandonment," Kali said calmly. "The reason it is so horrific is that when we really have it, down to our bones, we have abandoned the Goddess and ourselves."

PHONE SEX

Jasper had gone out of town, up north to teach a yoga workshop. Katrina thought she might be able to get some perspective while he was away but when he called her the first night she didn't hang up the way she had promised herself she would.

"I'm afraid you'll meet someone else," he said. "I've never been with a woman who likes sex as much as I do!"

"I'm not that desperate!"

"It's okay. I was always getting in trouble with my other girlfriends. Pawing them in the middle of the night the way you do with me. They were always having to push me off."

She wanted to hang up but he asked what she was wearing, where she was sitting. Then her hands were in her underpants.

After she came, he said, "I want to apologize again for hurting your feelings on the hike. You're beautiful. But no matter what I say about how beautiful you look, it really doesn't matter. You have to believe it for yourself."

Two nights later he called again. "I was going to go dancing but I decided not to."

"Why not?" she asked before she could stop herself.

"I don't want to get distracted by other women. This one girl here, from my workshop, she asked me to go. She's twenty-five and she's still a virgin. She wanted to talk to me about it. She realizes that there may be something wrong with her."

Where are you Zoloft, when I need you?

"Why do you have to tell me that, Jasper? Just don't say anything at all."

"But that would be lying!" His voice was shrill. "I am not going to hide my truth. I insist on sharing my truth with my partner. I will no longer be in a relationship of lies. If that's what you insist on, I'm afraid it's over."

Truth. What was truth? When was it important, essential? When was it better to avoid? Katrina realized she wasn't ready to let him go.

DIGGING UP THE LAWN

Scents of lavender massage oil, the summer flowers and wet grass through the window. Kali was massaging Katrina in the bedroom. Grace was playing with Sarah and Benji in the garden. The kids were running through the sprinklers and Katrina could hear their laughter as she lay under Kali's hands.

Kali was saying, "For now, maybe it's best for you to avoid sexual relationships altogether. Just heal yourself. Learn that you can survive alone, that you don't need a man to feel loved and beautiful."

From the garden, Katrina heard Grace say his name. Kali's eyes flashed darker.

Katrina put a kimono over her greasy shoulders and went into the garden .

Jasper looked thinner and his eyes older. He hardly glanced at Kali at all. He leaned down and kissed Katrina gently on her cheek. "I came to plant some flowers in your garden," he said. "I know you like flowers. And spring is coming."

"I wish you would call first."

"I did. No one answered."

"I mean, I wish you would let me know before you come by."

He just stood there, staring down at her. Zephyr was beside

the bigger dog, wagging his tail slowly from side to side. Bilbo and Frodo were giddily sniffing him, but he seemed oblivious to them.

"So, may I plant them? I'll have to dig up the lawn to make the beds."

And she said yes. Dig up my lawn.

Her friends left warily and Jasper put a blanket on the grass. He lifted Katrina in his arms and laid her gently on the blanket while he worked. She sat watching him, watching the sun sink lower in the sky. He used the hose to mark out the curved beds, then dug into the soil and placed flowers in. At one point he held up a small rose bush.

"Help me say a blessing on this one," he said.

Katrina came over and knelt beside him. She smelled the moist earth, the ragged roots, the fertilizer. A black bird on the telephone wire squawked down at them.

One for sorrow.

A blessing? The leaves of the rose bush were sparse and white-spotted.

"It's diseased," said Jasper, offering it up.

BLACK RIVER

It wasn't a bad dream. It only felt like one.

They drove all night. Blackness mostly, except for Las Vegas that slammed them with its lights and apparitions. New York, England, Paris, Rome, Egypt. *Where are we?* The little chapels advertising instant wedding bells at the outskirts of town. Less bright lights there. Crummy motels.

"I'll take you to the Luxor someday," Jasper said. "We'll drink ambrosia and see a show where the girls' skin is painted gold. I'll bathe you in rose water, rip the sheets with my teeth and wrap your naked body in strips of linen. Then I'll unwrap you slowly and fuck you with a cat watching from each post of the bed. We'll pretend to be dead and sleep in Tut's tomb."

But instead they passed through Vegas and stayed in a smelly motel and in the morning they met their group and got into a van and were driven to the dam. When Katrina had told Grace and Kali she was going kayaking they laughed, thinking it was a joke. When they realized she was serious they asked if she was sure she wanted to go through with it. She had paid for the trip right after she'd met Jasper. She had promised him she'd go. She regretted it but when she told him she had second thoughts, he said, "Have you ever imagined that a man might be able to take care of you? That you might be able to rely on someone, no matter what?"

Of course, he hadn't promised a thing but desire could make you delusional. Desire to be cared for. To rely, to be rescued.

She thought she was going to be in a kayak with Jasper but the guide said there were only single seat boats so she had to go alone. They sat her in the kayak in the middle of the wide river, dark from the shadows of the rocks on either side, and handed her the paddle.

She watched her boat rocking in the water, her arms jamming the paddle into the water, the kayak spinning in the wrong direction. Voices were yelling at her to come back but she kept moving farther away from the group. People were laughing.

"Get back here, darlin'," the guide yelled. He was a big, man, tan, strapping. When she'd first seen him, she felt safe. He would protect her if Jasper couldn't, right?

"Katrina, turn it around." She heard Jasper's voice.

She tried to yell back at them that she couldn't, but no words came out. She was moving farther and farther away.

"Get the fuck back here! Doesn't she hear me! Fuck!" The guide, Kent, was hollering louder now but the sound of rushing water was pounding in her head like blood.

"Fuck you!" she screamed. Finally. "I can't!"

Kent paddled over to her boat. "If you go down that way, you aren't coming back! That water'll take you!"

Her kayak rocked, water splashed over her legs. She could see ahead and to the side where the motion of the river sped up, frothed white with energy. The paddle flipped over from the force and she almost dropped it.

The guide finally managed to pull up alongside of her and herd her toward the shore, screaming the whole way. She didn't know what she did with the paddle to get herself out of the water. But finally she felt the solid thud of land. The sun seared her eyes. The water looked as black as its name.

Everyone else, including Jasper, was gone.

"Shit, woman, why didn't you listen?" Kent's moustache was so thick she couldn't see his mouth. It was spattered with wet drops that looked like spit.

"My friend told me we were going to be in a kayak together," was all she could manage to say. She looked around. Where was Jasper anyway? And everyone.

"They're back there," said the guide. "They stopped at some hot pools. We'll have to miss that. We'll start setting up camp."

"I'm not doing this anymore," she said. "I'm not going alone."

"We'll have to attach your boat to mine then for the rest of the trip," he said, handing her a shovel and a roll of toilet paper. "But you ain't getting a free ride, believe me. You'll work for your supper."

Jasper and the others came later. Katrina was huddling on the ground with her sleeping bag wrapped around her, drawing circles in the dirt with a stick.

"Are you okay, baby?" he asked. "I was worried."

Mute again.

"Kent said he'd hook you up to his boat for the rest of the trip. Let's take care of you now. Let's go bathe in some pools."

She followed him up the trail, over the shallow, gulping water. The pools were warm, bubbling among rocks that were shiny, slimy green and yellow with moss and lichen. She slipped a few times, bruising her knees and elbows but she didn't feel a thing. She was still checked out of her body, watching herself from a safe distance.

But nothing really felt safe. Signs along the creek trail warned against getting the water into your nose. There was some kind of deadly parasite that could enter your body that way.

"Is it okay?" she asked. "I mean, what if you inhale some by mistake?"

Jasper took off his clothes and slid into the pool. His body was distorted under the water, longer, wiggly and greenish-white.

"Just don't suck a bunch of water up there," he said. "I've done this a million times. It's perfectly safe."

She took off her shorts and T-shirt; her one-piece swimsuit was underneath. She hesitated at the edge of the water.

"You don't need clothes in here," Jasper said.

His body had disturbed dirt from the bottom so brown clouds erupted under the surface.

She watched herself stepping into the pool, crouching in the dirt, then sliding her shoulders under the warm surface. She stared down at her belly and thighs. They looked larger and paler than usual, distorted under the water.

"Look at the yoni!" Jasper exclaimed.

In the side of the rock was a cleft that did resemble a vagina between two voluptuous thighs. Jasper reached out and brought Katrina closer by sliding his hand into the leg hole of her one-piece.

That night they ate dinner by the campfire with the rest of the group. She could have sworn she'd read that vegetarian meals would be available but there was only grilled meat. When she asked the guide if she could have something else he handed her a package of pasta and a large pot.

"You can go down to the river and fill it for boiling. We're low on drinking water."

She thought about the parasites in the pools and ate a power bar she'd brought instead. After dinner someone began to drum and everyone danced by the fire. She sat drinking her beer, watching everyone dance through the shimmering screen of smoke. It looked as if the flames were leaping around their feet. The women were waving their arms above their heads and howling at the moon. One of them, a redhead, took off her top and fondled her breasts. Jasper whooped. Katrina got up and stumbled into the darkness of the bushes where she vomited up what little food she had in her stomach.

Jasper joined her in the tent a little while later. She was quaking with cold and the heat of his body was all she cared about. He slid his hand inside her sweat pants. She could hear the others laughing by the fire right outside.

"They'll hear," she said. She wished she could have said she was too tired but the truth was, she wasn't. She needed his fingers to help her sleep, there on the cold ground, pebbles digging into her already bruised flesh.

"They want to hear your pleasure," said Jasper.

He fell asleep with his hand inside her. She wiggled away from him and lay there beside him, unable to sleep. Her eye sockets itched. She listened to the campers disperse to their tents. She thought about the shovel stuck in the earth by the creek, the trek in the dark to get there.

She wasn't afraid, though. She was still far away, watching her hand patting the ground for the flashlight, her body crawling out of the tent, putting on her hiking boots, walking through the shallow, hissing snake of water to the shit hole by the side of the creek.

When she got back to the tent she lay next to Jasper, listening for rain, wondering how she could clamber up the sheer rock face in a flash flood. There would be no other escape.

She woke to the sun hitting the side of the tent and Jasper was gone; she smelled food and heard laughter. Everyone was already gathered around, eating pancakes.

Jasper was sitting in a camp chair. He didn't see her.

The red-haired woman and her friend came up to him, and the red-head said, "Get out of that chair, dude. It's the goddess chair."

"You're right," said Jasper. "It brought the goddesses right to me."

The women giggled. Jasper sauntered over to Katrina,

kicking the coals from the last night's fire with his boots.

"How'd you sleep? You look wiped."

"I'm okay," she muttered.

"What's wrong? Are you too much of a princess to rough it with me?"

She walked away to get some coffee. Jasper followed her.

"What?"

"So this is a goddess trip. I get it. No princesses allowed."

"I'm sorry, baby. I was just teasing you. We're going to have a good day today. We're going to find some hot pools and soak all day. And Kent said he'd hook you up to him again. Everything's going to be okay."

While she was paddling in the boat behind the guide's, he kept shouting back at her, "It's just like tantra. You can't work it too hard. Just relax into it, darlin, and you'll last for hours."

When they got to shore everyone else's kayaks were already there, haphazardly jammed against the rocks. Katrina and Kent hiked up to a giant waterfall, steamy hot, pouring off the green and yellow slimed rock face into the pool. The other campers were reclining in the brown water, their faces smeared with mud like some kind of earth spirits.

Kent took off his clothes and lumbered in. Jasper gestured for Katrina to come, too. She felt so visible, exposed on the sharp rocks, as she stripped down to her bathing suit. Everyone else was naked.

The redhead reached for a bottle of shampoo. She swam over to Jasper, straddled him and began washing his hair. The guide was massaging Katrina's feet. She let him. One of the women was floating on her back while four men held her limbs and a fifth supported her head. Katrina watched the nude, spread body, the calm face, floating hair, the exposed genitals. When someone asked if Katrina wanted a turn she declined.

"You're doing great," the redhead told her. "Not everyone is comfortable with their bodies."

"That didn't bother you, did it?" Jasper asked later when they were eating their sandwiches on the rocks. "Artemesia and me? You seemed busy with Kent."

"This isn't my scene, I guess," she said.

Some people aren't comfortable with their bodies.

"I'm sorry, baby. Let's just go off by ourselves. I enjoy being social more than you do but I also like to have some alone time. I heard there are some great pools higher up."

She followed him over the slippery rocks. She was still clinging to the fantasy that he could save her from her fears.

Somehow Artemesia had managed to beat them up the trail. She was still naked, her voluptuous ass perched on the rocks above as she struggled to climb the waterfall. Jasper stood below her. When she started to slip he caught her in his arms and she giggled. He was naked, too, except for the towel around his waist. Katrina felt dizzy with nausea.

She slid on the slimy rock and scraped her shin but she was too numb to feel anything and the blood surprised her, like someone else's.

Somehow, then, they were all in a pool together.

Artemesia was saying, "Tantra isn't really about sex, necessarily. It's about love. People just loving each other unconditionally, without the boundaries that divide us."

Jasper was saying, "I saw a yoni in the rock back at our camp. I'll show you tonight."

Katrina was saying nothing. She was realizing that none of this was Jasper's fault. The whole trip was like a dream, just a reflection of her fears. The problem was, her nightmares weren't like everyone else's—they came true.

I promised myself I would break up with Jasper when we got to L.A. But that night I dreamed that he had a black cat. I had to remove the cat's teeth, clean them, and put them back. The teeth were like tiny needles. I was very busy, working; I wasn't going anywhere yet.

EMOTIONAL LESBIAN

This is a lovely thing to remember:

Grace stepped out of the bathroom wearing a towel wrapped around her body. Her wet hair streamed down her shoulders.

"I was thinking," she said. "I think you need to take a break from relationships."

And Katrina hadn't even let Grace know what Jasper had said on the cliff. *I don't want to upset her,* she told herself. But maybe she just didn't want to face her own disgust reflected in Grace's face. She had told Grace a little about Black River, though. That was enough.

"I know. That's what Kali says. I'm a fucking connection junkie or something, you know? I mean what's my problem?"

"I wish I'd told you to get the hell out of there right away."

"But I don't want to go back to the land of the walking dead."

"Then maybe you need to have a relationship with a woman."

The afternoon sun was pouring in, lighting up the motes around Grace like fairy dust.

"I had this friend," she said, "from college. We saw each other up until the time I met Gerald, even while I was dating men. It was really beautiful and loving and safe."

Katrina couldn't believe it — mostly because she thought she knew everything about Grace. But she'd thought that before

Grace told her about the melanoma, too.

The pang of jealousy surprised her.

"Sometimes it's just better to be with a woman and not, you know, not have all the shit that goes along with the man thing."

"Well, I think I may have a crush on Kali," Katrina said, realizing that Grace didn't know everything about her, either. "I am such an emotional lesbian."

"Do you mean you are a lesbian emotionally or you are an emotional woman who is a lesbian? Because I already know that you are too emotional."

"Ha-ha. I just like women so much more than men in general. I guess I just was so captivated with this idea of an organ that can plant baby seeds in you. But women give me almost everything I need."

"Except a baby seed," Grace said.

"I wouldn't know what to do."

"That's not true" Grace said. "You've had about twenty years of experience unless you've never touched yourself. It's much easier than learning a whole different anatomy."

What I remember most about the conversation is this: Grace and I were giggling. She was naked, wearing only a towel, her wet hair streaming down her shoulders. The light streamed also, into the house lighting up the dust motes like glitter. I felt as if a grip on my throat had loosened. We were closer than we had ever been; we were happy.

Jasper was not there.

MERMAIDS

Grace and Katrina took Sarah and Benji to the natural history museum to see the exhibit on great civilizations that had come to cataclysmic ends. It was Grace's idea, a way to distract Katrina from Jasper. But when they got there Katrina started thinking about earthquakes. Grace said the exhibit also explained how some civilizations survived but Katrina still wasn't up for it and the kids wanted to see the animals so they did that instead.

They were in the long dark hall, the animals lit up in their cases. So strangely dead and alive at the same time. They had always disturbed Katrina, ever since she came there as a child with Lise.

Sarah and Benji were squealing about the dead mountain lions devouring a dead dead zebra. A dead zebra playing the role of a dead zebra. Grace and Katrina went to stand in front of the dead sea lions.

Their bodies were massive and furred against the blocks of fake ice. Their eyes were black glass. They were like huge dead imprisoned fur women. They made Katrina want to weep every time she saw them.

Grace put her arms around her. She had on a little crochet jacket Katrina had made. The sleeves were too long and draped over her hands.

"What is it about them?" Grace said. "They make the hair stand up on my neck."

"Me, too. Kali thinks it has to do with mermaids."

Kali believed that there were three tribes of women in what she called the Awakening Community. The fairies—that included mermaids, dryads and other spirits, the warriors and the priestesses. She said that Grace and Katrina were fairies, and that she, Kali was a warrior priestess. Supposedly Grace had a little more warrior in her than Katrina did.

"The warriors and the fairies don't always get along," Kali said. "They threaten each other in some primordial way. Fairies are the artists—super-sensitive; they react to everything by going inward, going underground, back into the earth. Warriors know how to be in the world, how to attack when they need to. The priestesses are here to bring them together. Ideally, we should be part of one tribe," Kali said," especially now in this world torn asunder."

Asunder. What a perfect word to describe us all.

"What about the men?" Katrina had asked Kali once.

"Their hearts are broken, too, but it's worse in a way."

"Why?"

Kali classified the men as elves, giants, warriors and priests. But she said that almost all were so out of touch with their origins that it became perverse.

"Most of them think with their penises; they don't even know their hearts are broken."

I didn't want to believe this. But, then—cancer, betrayal, tidal waves, hurricanes, earthquakes, war—there were many, many things about life I didn't want to believe.

WITCHES AND VAMPIRES

Katrina and Grace were dancing together in the dark when the woman came up to them. She took Grace's hands.

"You're so beautiful," she said.

Grace thanked her. People told Grace that all the time but she acted as if you were the first one who had ever said it. Not only because of how polite she was; it was as if she really didn't believe it herself.

"Please come with me," the woman said.

Katrina followed them into the front courtyard. For some reason, she thought she should be there in case Gracie needed help.

Not that I'm much help. With my mind full of fucked up dreams.

"You are so beautiful," the woman said again, "so full of light."

"Thank you. So are you!"

"Well, I can honestly say no one has ever told me I am so full of light. But… I saw something. I feel I have to share it. That it wouldn't be right not to tell you."

Katrina watched Grace's earnest, helpful, slightly worried expression, the tilt of her head, the squint of her eyes.

"I looked at you and saw a door shaped like a giant skull. And you. Wanting to leave."

Katrina grabbed Grace's arm and walked her back inside, away from this person. The room was dark, the air humid with sweat. Katrina hugged Grace and felt her heart through her dance camisole, so immediate, close to the surface.

You seem thinner, Katrina thought, but she didn't say it. *Don't get any thinner; you'll be gone. Maybe I'm just jealous.*

Jasper was standing there. He had promised to meet her at dance but he was an hour late.

"You need to be more grounded," he said, putting his arm around her shoulders. "I told you." He looked at Grace. "Both of you. That's how witches and vampires get in."

His birthmark seemed to pulse in the strobe light.

"Do you know that woman?"

"There is something really appealing for men about the damsel in distress thing," he said.

GRACE

Did I tell you that Grace fought melanoma twice? I like to forget about it. Pretend it never happened. Pretend it can never happen again. If Grace can manifest peonies and a house, a nearly seven foot tall husband and two beauteous children, she must be able to manifest a cancer-free body, right?

Moles just kept appearing. She treated it aggressively both times. People think she is this hardcore New Age nature girl but she went for the most intense Western medicine she could find. She said, "I'm going to kick that motherfucker cancer's ass."

Have I told you how much I love Grace? How she is the best friend? How she is the best mom in the world? How she is the best dancer not only because of her training but because of how much joy she expresses and how much she gives to her partner?

Love is the worst earthquake there is. It can crush you to the thickness of your bones. Love can be like cancer sometimes. Terminal. It can make you vomit. It can make you want to cut it out. It can take you over against your will.

"Katrina, it came back. There are more moles. I know they're it. They're going to cut me up again. They're going to make me lose my hair. Don't let them make me lose my hair."

She drove over to Grace and Gerald's house in Venice. The dream house that Grace manifested—white Craftsman with green trim, a white picket fence and a trellis covered with white roses, inside pale florals and light green velvet and a backyard with morning glories and jacaranda trees. Sarah and Benji were at nursery school and Gerald was at a meeting. Katrina took Grace in her arms and held her and they cried. It was just like when her mother said she had breast cancer. Hair and tears and heartbeats indistinguishable.

"I'm not going through the treatments," she said. "I can't. I can't let them cut out any more parts of me."

Katrina wanted to scream at her that she had to, what was she thinking, this was her life here. *And if you aren't worried about me, what about your babies?*

But Grace was going to Brazil to see a healer there. She had first heard about him on *60 Minutes*. Then some friends from dance told her how he'd helped their friends, she said.

"Who?" Katrina asked

"You don't know them."

I don't think she was giving up. It's just so hard to lose your hair again, your golden hair. It's so hard to be vomiting so fiercely when you are trying to care for babies looking at you with their eyes. More knives, more cutting. It's all so hard.

People always ask Grace—when they find out about her melanoma—they ask her, "Do you have a spiritual practice?" And she says, "I just dance."

People always say to Grace, "I wish I knew what to say." And Grace replies, in her most gentle, kind voice, as if reassuring them when they are trying to reassure her, "There's nothing really to say. Basically there is nothing to say about cancer except that it is fucked up."

Katrina begged to take a leave of absence from work and go with her but Grace wanted to be alone. She said she needed Katrina to stay and take care of Gerald and the kids.

I didn't like how she said that, as if she thought she wasn't coming back.

"You have to come back," Katrina said. "There is no way I am doing this life thing without you, mamacita."

"There is no way you aren't," said Grace. She wiped the globs of tears from her blue eyes and tried to smile. "I'll be back, man. Okay?

THE NEXT SIXTY YEARS
November 28, 2000

Grace told me today that she's pregnant. I was so happy for her. At first.

I went over there to celebrate but Gerald was looking miserable and I asked him what was wrong. He waited till Grace was out of the room and then he told me that the doctors had said she shouldn't try to have a baby. It might bring the cancer back, they said. But she'd done it anyway, intentionally, without telling him. She said having a baby was more important to her than anything.

"More than your life?" he had asked.

"More than anything, baby."

"More than me?"

Gerald said she hadn't answered that question at first. Then she'd said, "You will always have our child."

"I want you," he told her.

"I'll be okay. How could I not? When I see the baby's face I'll know I have to be around for at least the next twenty years."

"Sixty years," said Gerald.

"Yeah, sixty. And, besides, I can't let you raise her by yourself. You're too absent-minded."

And that was the end of their discussion.

"'What are you going to do?" I asked Gerald.

"I'm going to say the serenity prayer as much as I need to, help her through the pregnancy, fall in love with our child and pretend I never heard what the doctors said."

And from then on, he never mentioned it again.

SARAH AND BENJI

While Grace was away, Jasper left, too. He said, "It's probably better that we don't try to talk on the phone. It got us into trouble last time. Let's just email."

Katrina agreed. She was relieved actually.

She spent her free time with Sarah and Benji. She made lists of things to do with them. Travel Town to ride the trains, the petting zoo and pony rides at the farmer's market, the La Brea tar pits, the museum. One day she took them to the Santa Monica pier. Benji had on his Spiderman T-shirt and Sarah wore a tiara and a dress-up bridal gown over blue jeans tucked into ladybug rain boots, though the day was bright. They rode the glossily frosted-looking carousel; Sarah wanted a white horse and Benji a brown. Katrina stood between them, her hands on their waists. Sprigs of orange and blue and white painted flowers, flashing mirrors, tinkling music.

I wish I could make their lives like this.

After they'd gone around four times she bought them French fries and ice cream cones. She knew Grace tried to feed them better, didn't usually do fried or dairy, but their eyes were so sad and Katrina wanted to see them light up, even for a few moments. They played at the beach park until the sun was a low red ball hovering above the bloody waves. Katrina imagined thousands of dead mermaids. The moon was visible, too. A thin crescent like a primitive weapon. Sarah came and tucked herself into Katrina's lap.

"The sun is God's crown. The moon is God's wand."

"That's beautiful, Sarah."

"I miss my mommy."

Benji joined her. Katrina made space for him, too.

"I know, sweetie," she said. "She misses you guys. She'll be back soon."

"Mommy said that God would watch over us." Benji was holding Katrina's fingers so hard they hurt.

"That's true." Katrina gulped down a lump of sand in her throat. "God and maybe Goddess and me and your daddy. Until she gets back."

"God lives inside our hearts to help us when we are sad," he assured her.

They huddled together, leaning back, looking up at the darkening sky. The air was cooling off and Katrina was glad of the children's warmth against her.

"Kat, what is it when the sun and moon are together?" said Sarah.

"What, honey?"

"When the sun and moon are together God comes up."

"So God must be here now."

"The world is God's globe," Benji said.

THE SOFT UNDERBELLY

Grace came back from Brazil before she had a chance to see the healer because she couldn't eat or go to the bathroom. She checked into a hospital in the valley and she didn't have to refuse any treatments because it was too late.

Katrina sat beside her and held her hand. Lying there with her wispy, pale hair and slight body she looked like a child.

"I'm not scared anymore," she said. "It's more Gerald. Knowing he has to go through this. Not my kids, so much. They'll forget me eventually."

"Don't say that! No, they won't! Gracie, you're their mother."

"No," she whispered. *And this is when I knew it was over.* "You are."

Katrina brought groceries and babysat while Gerald was with Grace. Sarah and Benji looked different—suddenly older. Katrina read them stories and took them to the park and they didn't ask her the questions that she was braced for every time. She imagined that if she were Grace she would have wanted them next to her every second but it was also easy to understand that Grace couldn't bear to see what she loved most. What she didn't love felt safer.

Gerald called Katrina. His voice sounded shredded, small, too small for such a big man.

"Gerald? Is she okay?" Katrina sounded different, too. She could feel the hysteria welling up inside of her. Tried to choke it down.

"That friend of yours. He's been coming to see her in the hospital."

"What?"

"I found him over there today. Doing some kind of chakra healing. He's been doing it for a while she said. He's the one that helped arrange for her to go to Brazil. She didn't want to tell me."

"Let me talk to her."

"She's sleeping."

When they did talk, Grace sounded as different as Gerald had. She sounded hollow.

"I'm sorry if it upsets you."

"When did this happen?"

"He got in touch with me the day I saw the new moles. It was like he knew. Right after we saw him at dance. And that woman, with the skull door thing. And he told me about Brazil..."

"How can you let him get close to you?"

"You did."

"I needed him then."

"Your clock is ticking, Katrina. But it isn't going to fucking explode."

Grace woke in the night in the hospital with pains in her chest. It's impossible to imagine how much it hurt. When they looked, the doctors found tumors on her heart. I didn't know there could be tumors on someone's heart. Especially that heart. None of the disasters I had ever dreamed were this.

Grace went back to her dream house in Venice. Katrina wanted to fill it with peonies but she didn't. She didn't want to remind Grace or herself of the word "manifest." The house, Gerald, Benji and Sarah were reminders enough.

OVER

Living in Quakeland, I am a masochist. But think of our sunshine, ocean, flowers, canyons, museums, carousels, our gold-leaf light. I am only self-destructive to a certain degree.

"Let's face it, I don't want to be cruel but you obviously are poisoned with self hatred. And no matter how much a man falls in love with you, he won't be able to convince you that you aren't ugly and fat in his eyes or that he wants you more than anyone else. This is the truth. You need to face the truth."

That was what Jasper told Katrina when he came to her door and she asked why he hadn't told her about Grace.

"You want to hear every truth?" she said. "You want to hear the way I really feel about your penis?"

"My lingam is also an expression of my truth," said Jasper. "It recognized the hunger in your lower chakra and withdrew. You are always so highly lubricated and it will be impossible for anyone to get enough friction until you calm yourself."

"Leave now," she told him.

"I've come to get my things, actually."

He had a shirt and a toothbrush, shampoo, dog food, Zephyr's bowl, and a skillet. Katrina had already put them into a bag, along with the silver ring he had given her.

Sarah ran up and took Katrina's hand. "Come paint my face. I want to be the purple fairy! Benji wants to be Thomas the Tank Engine."

"Okay, honey, just a second."

Jasper stopped in the doorway. "Katrina, I hate to tell you this but I want you to know that you will never find anyone else like me. Who else will come to plant flowers in your garden? Who else will cry with you as if it is their own pain? Who else will lick away your tears and be willing to pleasure you as much as I do? You are going to regret this. But I see you are a very different person than who I thought you were. And now I want you to know without a doubt that it's over."

Sarah looked up at Katrina with a big question in her eyes. Katrina's hands were clapped over her ears and they were shaking so hard she could see Sarah's head move, so she let go and picked her up in her arms.

TSUNAMI WITH LEGS

We met on the day of the tsunami. At the time I took this as a positive portent, a good omen. Passion and not destruction. They don't seem so different after all.

As soon as Jasper left, the dreams of the world came back. So was he a shaman protecting me from my nightmares or just the supreme distraction: my walking tsunami sent to make me forget the one made of water?

A BRAIN IN A ROOM

It was lying on the floor, a fatty, throbby mass. And I knew, somehow, that it had been blown into the room from an explosion in the street. I knew there was going to be another bombing somewhere in the world but who would take me seriously? There were bombings reported almost every day. And I didn't know where the room was. Or to whom that brain belonged.

Other dreams: A ferry boat, painted beautiful colors—grass green, sky blue, lily orange—garlanded with flowers that I can actually smell. It is as sharp a smell as it is sweet. Women and children are on the deck singing as they sail to their place of worship. Deities are lined up along the outside of the ship. Blue Krishnas, goddesses with many arms, sacred cows with garlands. Tiny lights strung along the boat flash on and off, on and off. I am in a little rowboat, trying to shout a warning to the people on the ferry but they don't hear me.

I am sleeping in a gymnasium, in the dark with a lot of other people. In the other room I hear a voice rumbling. It is the voice of pure menace, hate and destruction. I know it is threatening all of us in this place but I can't move, I can't speak, I can't wake anyone to warn them. And then it's too late.

A woman is clawing through the rubble of her house to find something. I know with the sick knowing of my dreams that she is looking for her child, the one she admonished never to go outside when the high winds came. The obedient child who listened to her warnings about winds and stayed inside the house.

I went out and finally bought the earthquake supplies I'd been meaning to get for years. Canned food, batteries, extra water. I planned my escape routes and found my "triangles of life." But this didn't make the dreams stop either.

And I lie in my bed with them. I have to touch myself to make them stop. In this way they have become my lovers.

This is the worst one: Sarah and Benji are huddled in my arms, crying in fear. I can feel the wetness of their tears; I can smell their hair—they still have that sweet baby smell. "I will find you again," I tell Grace's children. "No matter what or how. I will always find you." In the dream I love them as though they are mine; their mother is not there.

NO ONE KNOWS WE ARE HERE

Katrina went to see Kali. She answered the door barefoot, in her kimono, smelling of rose oil that was slightly cloying, too sweet.

"Come in, lovey."

They sat drinking tea on Kali's cushions. The way the light filled the room made everything shine like amber.

No one knows we're here.

Katrina started talking; she couldn't stop. The therapists and the corresponding men. Her mother. Grace. Her dad. She had tried to find him once, on the internet, after her mother was diagnosed. She got back a formal email from a woman saying that Guru G. was in no way related to Katrina and that her pursuit of the matter would lead to legal action.

Finally she blurted out, "Once Jasper told me he was attracted to you. After that party. And I went crazy."

"You're so sensitive, lovey. Men just say shit."

"It made it worse because I get so possessive of you for some reason. I love you so much."

"I love you, too, darling," Kali said blandly.

"No, I mean I love you. I have a crush on you, almost."

Why was I telling her this? I felt so spun out from Jasper. Like I wanted to say everything on my mind, dance out every emotion I felt in public.

Kali used her yoga teacher voice. "That is so sweet of you," she said.

"You're just afraid," said Kali.

KATRINA

I had never been to New Orleans but people always told me how I would love it. The old mansions draped in moss, the secret gardens behind iron fences, the graveyards and music and dancing in the streets and carnival costumes and Cajun spices and the creatures of darkness. I couldn't watch the devastation on the news. I couldn't recall if I had had a premonition in a dream. All I really knew was that the city was gone, people were dead, and the hurricane had my name.

And Grace died.

She let them into her bed—Katrina and Gerald and Sarah and Benji—all of them squeezed into her dream bed with the white tulle draped over the top. She let them hold her and cry with her and she had said I love you and good-bye. They doctors had found the right narcotic—she hadn't been in too much pain at the end. That is how death is supposed to be, right? Inevitable, not too much pain, and your loved ones at your side.

But death is not supposed to happen to a dancer in her thirties with three year old twins; death from skin cancer is not supposed to happen to anyone's best friend.

(It has to happen to someone's best friend.)

One other thing—maybe Grace was delirious then but she had leaned over and whispered to Katrina, "Gerald felt like Jasper and I... like it was a betrayal. I wanted him to. So he can move on more easily. He loves you, man. You'll help him..."

Gerald is one of the tallest men I have ever seen. Kali said that is the prototype of the priest-giant. Not only his size, but his kindness and his heart. He has straight, shiny black Native American hair, Irish blue-steel eyes, an angular face and slightly pock marked cheeks. One of those faces that they always cast as villains in the movies. And then you see interviews with the actors and you can't believe that they are really these gentle men. Gerald was successful with those kinds of roles for a few years and then he wrote a screenplay and it was produced and he gave up acting altogether. His scripts are original and strange and magical—the kinds of things you don't think Hollywood would ever make but they do and people love them. The man is like something out of one of his movies. Even his childhood—growing up on a ranch with five brothers, abused by his father, loved by his mother who died mysteriously and suddenly. And every heroine in every script is another part of Grace. If I had ever met a man worthy of her, it was Gerald. How will he write this disaster to make it go away? How can I begin to help him?

She left Gerald and Sarah and Benji and went home. She was going to go back on the Zoloft as soon as she could get a prescription. No more orgasms? No more dreams, no more disasters, maybe a little numbness for the pain. Easy trade.

But Katrina didn't help Gerald and the drug didn't help her. She lay in front of the TV waiting for the Vitamin Z to kick in. Sometimes she'd have to turn the television off because there were news announcements that matched the dreams she'd already had. Like the London bombing where someone found a brain blown into a room from the street.

A man in a hat walks toward me, his arms outstretched, his face elongated with sorrow. He is the ghost Kali saw in my house. His hands are full of plants, their roots clumped with mud, severed from the earth, their leaves spotted with disease.

The group email from Jasper came a week later. It had pictures of Grace attached. Katrina didn't understand at first how he had those pictures at all. It was almost like seeing a ghost.

She was smiling, dancing, wearing her pretty clothes. Crisp white dresses she'd made from linen lace tablecloths, the tiny crochet sweater with sleeves that draped down over her hands, long gauze skirts, low slung baggy army pants cut off at the knee, men's tank tops she'd decorated with sequins, high wedge espadrilles that laced up her legs. At Katrina's party, in front of the dance studio, in the garden. And another picture: Grace at the end, very ill. But she was smiling. Katrina hadn't seen her smile like that in months. She was in bed. A bed with tie-dyed sheets and a purple comforter with a yin/yang symbol on it. There was a shirt, too. The blue sueded silk one, draped over Grace's bare shoulders.

One more picture: A crowd of people jammed into a room. You could make out a bald child and an emaciated man in a wheelchair. You could tell, somehow, that this was not Quakeland, not even America. This was a foreign place. And Grace was there, waiting with the people. She was in a wheelchair. Someone would have had to be pushing it. She had on a sweatshirt, her jeans, that looked too big for her, and her travel backpack was in her lap. The one she took to Brazil. Someone took this picture. Someone who was with her. Not a stranger.

The message read —

Dear Friends:

I consider you a friend if you receive this. I have spent the last few days joyously celebrating the life of my friend Grace, a beautiful dancer. Here are a few memories I have collected of her. I feel the blessing of her disease, in spite of how horrible it was, because it allowed me to get close to her. Her beauty and gracefulness will live on forever.

> Hugs,
> Jasper

JASPER

Jasper wore a red poncho. He was loping around the dance floor, spreading his arms like wings.

"I'm so sorry, Katrina," he said, reaching out for her. He looked too tall and his eyes scared her. She stumbled backwards "I'm sorry, I just can't play these childish games of pretending we don't know each other."

"Why did you do that? Why didn't you leave her alone? She wasn't your friend!"

"Katrina," Jasper said, "I always thought that was a perfect name for you but I didn't know why before." And he danced away.

That was when she knew she wanted to kill Jasper.

She heard his voice then.

"Grace!" he cried out. "Grace, baby, come back to us. Come back."

Kali had told her that you have to be careful not to call back spirits that have gone before their time. Because they may try to come. And it will be worse for them. And the portals will open for other spirits—the ones you don't want.

Katrina huddled into a ball on the floor. She didn't care if someone trampled her. She would have welcomed it.

Then she heard another voice, a woman's voice, a voice she

knew.

"Grace," the woman said, "we love you. And we know that you have followed the path you had to follow and we are filled with sorrow but we release you to your higher place, along with all the spirits for whom we long."

Katrina looked up and she hadn't dreamed it—Kali was standing there, in the center of the room, her hair falling blackly around her shoulders like raven's wings. Everyone was watching her. She walked over to Katrina and sat beside her and folded her up in her arms. Every muscle could be discerned under the taut caramelized color of her flesh.

"Lovey," Kali said contentedly, "I am going to kill that man."

When Katrina looked across the room she saw Jasper lying in a ball on the floor the way she had been. His back was shaking with sobs.

The thing is, I knew Grace, how she could affect you, no matter who you were.

I hated Jasper but I didn't blame him.

KALI

She did a past life regression for Katrina and Jasper. The women sat face to face in Kali's studio, with a candle burning between them. But this time Katrina had no thoughts of proclaiming her love. It felt as if there was no love inside of her to speak of.

This is what Kali saw:

Jasper and I are jousting, sparring with swords. We are us and not us. We are equally matched. I am almost the same height as he is, the same size. And we are doing tricks, some kind of magic. There are flowers growing and animals appearing and women disappearing. There is silk fabric covered with silver stars and strange symbols. There are potions, spells, illusions, enchantments.

But then, something happens.

What?

"He stabbed you", Kali said calmly. "In the heart."

"Don't tell me that," I said. "I can't think like that. I can't believe I was letting myself be a victim then, too.

Kali paused, then said, "But the thing is, you wanted him to do it. You told him to do it. It was because the pain of separation was too scary, too out of your control. The separation we all always experience with each other. So you thought if he killed you, there would be less pain, you see? And he was angry at you for asking him to do it. He felt you were controlling him; that he couldn't say no."

I felt nauseous, chills chasing each other up my back and across the nape of my neck.

I wanted to scream at Kali, tell her to shut up. Why was she saying this? But the thing was, it felt so real. It felt so true and I could even remember it. And metaphorically at least, it was the truth. It felt as if we had re-enacted the whole thing on the cliff, with a hand instead of a sword. The wound to the lower chakras rather than my heart. The drama no longer larger than life, tragic, beautiful. Just two messed up people fucking around on a cliff.

"I am going to ask you to cancel some contracts," Kali said. "I want you to envision the words I say written on a piece of paper and I want you to envision yourself taking a stamp and canceling what is written there, if you are willing. Then I want you to imagine yourself tearing up the contract and throwing it on the pyre."

Katrina nodded, feeling dazed, watching the flame sputter too high. *We should have cut the wick,* she thought. Kali spoke quickly, hardly taking a breath.

"Are you willing to cancel the contract that says you are only a woman if a man perceives you as desirable?

"Are you willing to cancel the contract that says you are not entitled to true love?

"Are you willing to cancel the contract that says you will always be the second choice?

"Are you willing to cancel the contract that says you are a victim?

"Are you willing to cancel the contract that says you are doomed never to consummate your truest passion?

"Are you willing to cancel the contract that says in order to be loved you must be weak?

"Are you willing to cancel the contract that says you must suffer for love?

"Are you willing to cancel the contract that says that your well-being must be determined by the actions of others?

"Are you willing to cancel the contract that says your soul children must come to you in only one way, or you will not receive them?

"Are you willing to cancel the contract that says if your loved ones are taken from you, you too must leave this place?"

They were all easy to cancel, at least on the surface. Except the last one.

When my mom died, I wanted to go, too. It seemed natural to me at the time. She had always been my best friend. It was Grace who found me then, in a dance class I had dragged myself to. It was Grace who kept me here.

Jasper was like the skull in the door beckoning me to leave.

"There are spells I know," Kali said. "Spells of destruction. They leave no trace. Bones make good adornments."

Katrina grabbed her arm, around her bicep where the snake was tattooed. She felt the muscle tighten under her grip. Kali's skin was hot but cold shot through Katrina's fingertips, toward her chest.

"I don't want to hurt him. My God, Kali. Fuck."

Kali was weeping; Katrina had never seen her cry before. Never. Not even when she heard about Gracie. Not a single tear.

"I can't believe she's dead," Kali said. "And all these useless motherfuckers are running around with their heads stuck up their asses trying to destroy the planet. Or not hurting Gaia but just picking a few women they can fuck around with instead. I mean, believe me, why do you think I needed that snake? My boyfriend was sleeping with five women when he was with me. He couldn't get it up for me because he was sticking his dick into five other women. And I loved him so much I didn't care. Because all I wanted was a baby. That was all I wanted. Just like you. And now it's too fucking late for both of us."

Katrina held Kali in her arms. Her mother was gone. Grace was gone. Kali Kalifornia, the beautiful, the destroyer, was all she had left.

VENICE

Grace had always wanted to live in Venice. Even as a child, growing up in Massachusetts she imagined it.

She didn't think about a sky without ozone, a virulent, violent sun.

She had heard about the colonnade by the sea, the houses on canals, and the way the ducks paraded through the yards. She liked the idea of ramshackle beach cottages with peeling paint, bamboo fences, and wildflower gardens. The artists and the surfers. Grace learned to surf in Venice. She danced to African drums on the boardwalk, rode a bike, roller-skated, roller-bladed, bought crochet string bikinis, had her face painted, got henna tattoos. She met Gerald at a poetry reading at Beyond Baroque. On their first date, after brunch at the Inn of the Seventh Ray, they built a sandcastle and watched the sun set. Just a few months later they rented a tiny apartment on the boardwalk and then the house where Katrina now lived, until they could afford their home.

There was a memorial for Grace in that home, in the backyard with the jacaranda trees. No one could manage the sight of peonies so there was every other kind of flower. There were photos of Grace everywhere. No one could really handle that either. A little tow-headed girl, as a long-legged teenager, a dancer, a bride with tea roses in her hair, a mommy with a babe at each breast.

Grace's parents were there. Katrina had met them before but they seemed not to know who she was. They looked like tanned, well-dressed and coiffed sleepwalkers.

The day was hot, too hot. The air swelled with heat. Everyone seemed dazed, wandering around or huddled together with puffy faces. Sometimes they would flirt or laugh, and then they would get quiet again, disgusted with themselves. *But Grace would have wanted them to flirt and laugh*, Katrina thought. *And dance, especially to dance. There are two kinds of people—those who want you to dance at their funeral, and those that don't.* Finally someone started beating on some drums and they did dance, then, for Grace. Later, they would all go down to the ocean and strip off their clothing (even Katrina, forgetting her body) and dance into the waves.

Kali wasn't there. She had moved up north suddenly, to Santa Cruz, saying only a quick goodbye. She had given Katrina a small wooden rattle in the shape of a snake before she left. Katrina wondered if she would ever hear from her again.

Jasper tried to come in but Gerald's A.A. buddies and brothers were standing at the front door in their black suits and ties, and they called Gerald and he looked down at Jasper and sent him away. He not only told Jasper not to come back there; he told him never to contact Katrina again.

I didn't need him to do it. By then I was strong enough, recovering Quakeland daughter, to have sent him away myself. I had already lost what was most precious to me and survived.

135

NEW ORLEANS

"Write them down," Grace said. *"Like Anne Frank had Kitty. I'll be your Kitty. Write them to me."*

Dear Grace:

The cars are floating in a swamp of water. A woman is sitting on the roof of one of the cars. The water is a red so dark you might call it black.

And then, the woman kneels down and puts her face to the surface of the water. She begins to drink.

You and I are walking down a tree-lined street. There are old moss-draped homes with big front porches and iron railings. Phosphorescent lights shine in the windows. Music in the air. A parade. People dressed as Wild Things, Mad Hatters, March Hares, Queen of Hearts, Hobbits, lions, ice witches, fairy princesses, goblins, ballerinas, superheroes. They dance along, dance past us, in slow motion, waving and smiling. You take my hand.

"Isn't it beautiful?"

"Where are we?"

"New Orleans," you say. *"I always wanted to go…"*

"Are we helping her?" I ask.

"No, babe," you say. *"She's helping us."*

THE L.A. LABYRINTH

In the hills above Malibu was an old monastery. The rambling buildings and tiled courtyards were once a mansion built by a woman and abandoned when her husband-to-be suddenly died. You could see the sun winking on the ocean waves and, at night, through the fog, the lights of the city from the gardens. Fountains tinkled merrily, and the air smelled of salt and roses. An old German Shepherd chased a ball, and people on retreat ate scrambled eggs in the dining hall and sat on stone benches watching the sun rise.

Katrina went there by herself after Grace. Before she left, Kali had told her about a labyrinth. When she heard the word, Katrina imagined high walls of stone or hedges in which to lose herself but it was just a circle of carefully placed stones, on the top of the hill among the roses. You were supposed to walk it with a meditation in your mind, a prayer of some kind.

Her instinct was to pray for her perfect partner, someone who would take away the pain of Grace's death, take her out of the disaster of her own mind. But just as she entered the little mandala above her fragile, glamorously polluted city, two words came into her head. Love was only the second.

The first was Self.

SARAH AND BENJI
May 28, 2001

Sarah Emily Powers and Benjamin Dashell Powers were born today. Grace struggled through the entire night but when it was over I've never seen her so happy. She was just shining. I look at their tiny, squashed, red faces, their bright, myopic eyes and wrinkly fingers and toes. I want to love them. Am I jealous because of my miscarriage and because I want at least one of my own before it's too late? Am I angry that she made this choice without thinking of her husband, or me? Am I afraid they will take her away from me in more ways than one? It's as if Gerald really has forgotten what the doctors said. But he is under the baby-spell Maybe, someday, I will be able to forget, too.

SAFE
September 11, 2005

Dear Grace:

Something has changed.

I am not outside of myself, detached, writing the story, watching the play. I am as alive as I used to feel only in my dreams.

Sarah and Benji are staying over tonight, curled up like kitties in my bed. The pillows are damp and chamomile-scented from their hair because I washed it in the tub before we went to sleep. Not damp from their tears, although there are nights, many nights, when this is the case.

The other morning, though, they both woke up smiling.

"You look so happy, Pooh-bears!" I said.

"Mommy cameded last night," Benji told me.

"Yes! Mommy was here!" his sister said.

I am sure that you are not a ghost but ascended, my darling.

Before we fell asleep I told them a story about a girl who has a ballerina inside her heart, who teaches her how to dance, and a boy with a superhero inside of him. They asked me to turn the story into a book with pictures. Maybe I will.

We prayed, too. Kneeling at the foot of the bed. We each took a turn and then repeated each other's. Benji's prayer was, "Piderman. Batman. Superheroes." Sarah's prayer was, "When you die, you go inside God's lap."

In the morning I will take her to ballet at the recreation center in the park and Benji to the train store in the 1920's building that looks like a station. Then we will go to the Santa Monica pier and ride the carousel as many times as they want.

The dogs sleep peacefully at the foot of the bed; I can hear their steady breath. I step carefully over them and go into the kitchen; moonlight seeps through the glass windowbox full of orchids and herbs. The orchids look like sticks with leaves but I water them for ten minutes every week like you told me and feed them every two and I know there will be buds in the spring. This house is a little plantland. There are clever green vines tendrilling their way through the spaces around the windows, climbing the walls inside the house! I go out into the yard. Lemon blossoms and jasmine sweeten the air. The white light filters down through the trees onto my skin. Even the diseased rose bush that Jasper planted produced a red rose today.

For now there is still a war but there are no tidal waves, witches, stabbings, no holocausts, hurricanes, earthquakes, tumors right here. Maybe ghosts, but gentle ones. Maybe not ghosts at all, but ascendant beings. My garden spirit and you, waltzing together on the lawn. There are no disasters here tonight; the world is not coming to an end. In Quakeland, city poised to fall into the sea, my home stands solid. Even the home of my body. My soul children are in my bed dreaming of their dancing mommy. In this way, for now, we are safe.

In Her Own Words

When she was asked to write a story about me, I said to the woman, "Tell them I have insomnia. I don't sleep most nights. I toss my everycolor hair. The lights hurt my eyes. I have a perpetual sunburn. Nothing cools me off. So much is happening all over my body. So many stories. Births and tumors. Would you be able to sleep if you were me? Ask them that."

Van Nuys

Grace is dying. She is only thirty-three. Blond. Thin. Tan. Everyone here wants to look like that. A modern dancer. When she dances, people think, "See how she moves? So true to herself. I know that no matter what, if I come if I go, she will still be there, moving from her center. From her authenticity." Grace has a tall husband with a somber face. She has twins with perpetually messy hair and sleepy eyes. They have the lovely, bewildered look of babies having to grow up all at once.

It is not right that this should be happening to them. But what can I do? I am just a crazy city without enough ozone.

Grace checked herself into a hospital in Van Nuys after she got back from Brazil.

I'm not proud of Van Nuys. The air stinks. The light is smog-colored. There is a flatness to everything—the light, the sky, the landscape. Where are the hills? The trees? Grace wants to be back home in Venice but she is also afraid to be in a place she cannot imagine leaving. Morning glories entwined with bamboo. Morning-glory-colored sky. Sea smell. Sand in all the sheets. Found shells trying to keep their luster in a bowl of water on the front step. Soon, they will take her there.

Grace traveled to Brazil to see a healer but she came back with crystals for her friends and more tumors. Too many to do anything about. She woke in the night with palpitations and when they checked her heart there were tumors there, too. On her heart.

I keep thinking about this. Grace. Tumors. Heart. Melanoma. No ozone.

The therapist went to visit her. She gave him a crystal from Brazil. He sat beside her and talked to her in a soft voice. I was glad he was there.

Venice

I am proud of Venice. This is where the therapist lives, on the canals. He has a dusky purple and green Craftsman house, the same colors as the garden. Princess flowers, lavender, wisteria, sage, rosemary. Inside the paintings are of mythical subjects. Cupid and Psyche. Venus. Nymphs. Pygmalion. In this last one, the woman is coming to life at the man's touch, but he has also created her exactly as he wants her to be. All the women in the paintings look pale and full. There is a red velvet couch and a pomegranate red oriental carpet with gold flecks. There are always flowers on the table. The therapist is adding onto the house. He is putting in a larger bedroom and bath, and a hot tub outside near the gazebo. His office, the place where he sees his clients, is in the back.

The therapist was living with a young woman who left him. Let's call her "the girlfriend." I don't want to tell you the story because it is private and I don't want him to feel I have been too invasive. After she left he mourned for a long time.

Now this other woman has found him. She comes over every weekend and lies on the couch beside him. The light is soft, filtering at just the right angle through the large front window. She used to be afraid someone would see them sitting there, half-dressed. But now she hardly notices if the curtains are open or closed. The light soothes and entrances her. She feels so comforted here. As if she was supposed to have arrived all along.

While they are making love, they talk about everything. She feels like a Georgia O'Keefe painting, all those layers unfolding, all those walls opening, all that color and vibrance. She wants him to put his fingers inside of her all the time. She wants to expose all the parts of her body to him. Up close he resembles a lion with a craggy face. His body is young and muscular. She would cry all the time but she is on anti-depressants like all the girls in my stories so her tears are rare. It feels like she is watching her life through a sheer scrim. She can't come easily either, because of the medication. He is patient, watching her face, listening to her breath, touching her every way he can think of. She is wet almost all the time, in a perpetual pre-orgasmic state. He tells her he likes it, but sometimes she is too wet for the right friction. Sometimes she has to go home and finish it off because she doesn't want his hand to get tired. This is irrelevant. Emotionally it feels as if she is always having orgasms in his arms.

Culver City

The woman moved into a house in Culver City with her two young children. If you look closely you can see that the house is painted a very pale green. The waxy-leaved vines growing up the wall are trying to make the house greener. The woman put a Buddha statue among the white, red and orange roses.

I like this part of Culver City. The woman can walk her

children to their pre-school instead of having to get in her car. The pre-school is in an old stone building at the edge of the park. The park is a little rectangular island among all the houses. Large trees with pale, peeling bark make soft shadows on the lawn. On the Fourth of July people put out their picnic blankets and watch fireworks from the park. The woman can see them from her bedroom window. On one of their first dates, while her children were with their father, the therapist made love to her standing at the window while they watched the sky ejaculating colors.

The woman can also walk over a bridge, over the creek, to the library and to a little coffee house and a nail salon. I didn't mean to become so ruled by automobiles. I like when people can walk. Culver City has a nice downtown area with a farmer's market, a sweet, very yin yoga studio, a Trader Joe's, a Starbucks, restaurants, and galleries. The Culver Hotel has the look of a haunted building, tall and angular on a corner. The actors who played the Munchkins from *The Wizard of Oz* stayed there when they were filming. There is an old gentleman who sits outside all night long, with his computer, working. He's probably writing a screenplay. Culver City was originally going to be named "Filmville" because of all the studios. You've got to love that. Filmville.

In spite of all the nice things about Culver City, the woman's children say the same thing everyday: "We want to live with you and Daddy." The woman repeats, over and over again, like a mantra, so she doesn't have to really hear what she is saying, "I know this is so hard for you and I'm sorry and Daddy and I get along better this way, in two houses." Because their parents no longer fight, because they no longer have chronic headaches and stomachaches, the children accept this. They know it is the truth.

But the woman misses them when they are away. She misses them so much that she has to take a sleeping pill when they aren't with her. Otherwise she wakes all night, patting the sheets, looking for them, panicking, not remembering why they are gone.

West Los Angeles

Every weekend, when her ex-husband has the kids, the woman goes to a fencing studio across the street from Bed, Bath and Beyond, in that vague place called West Los Angeles, to dance. There is a large room with international flags all over the walls. The floor is old, beaten up, with jagged edges that can tear your feet. About a hundred people shake and sweat for three hours. This is where the woman originally met the therapist. She tried to dance with him but he would not meet her eyes. He kept his head lowered and his shoulders squared. She thought he was handsome but unapproachable. Later, he told her he was grief-stricken from his break-up. He told her she seemed flighty and trendy in her tie-dyed pants.

She sometimes ran around the room because she felt she had so much pent-up energy that needed to be released. In her marriage she hadn't had sex for almost three years. The therapist told her she seemed to be running from herself. That no matter how fast she ran, everything would still be there.

Once, many months after their first dances, she slowed down, he opened his eyes, and they met. There was a Sinead O'Connor song playing and he whispered the lyrics to the woman as he held her. He lifted her in his arms and cradled her. She closed her eyes and collapsed against him. He held her upside down and over his back. It was something different, something scary and seductive and compelling, to dance like this. She mistook the therapist's gestures and whispers for some kind of love, even though she had seen other people do this, and then walk away from each other, without even knowing each other's names.

Still, something was real. She trusted him.

Santa Monica

This is where the woman's ex-husband lived when she met him. He had a single apartment near Main Street. No kitchen, a hotplate in the bathroom, his L.A. mystery paperbacks on the shelves. He worked in the evenings so she would get a video at Vidiots and some Ben and Jerry's ice cream, and wait for him. The ocean air smelled so good—so close and tangible with salt. And the jasmine that grew up the wall. Sometimes the woman couldn't wait and she masturbated so when he came home she told him that was why she wasn't able to have an orgasm. They never had sex in the light. They never talked during sex. Now they just don't talk. At this time in their relationship, though, the woman was happy. She and her ex-husband had both wanted the same thing—babies. They even had independently picked the same names, male and female, before even having met each other.

Santa Monica. Almost ten years later. The Church in Ocean Park. The woman went to a dance there. The therapist was walking in at the same time. His voice was soothing. "It's less of a scene here," he promised her, when she said the other dance place was freaking her out with everyone rolling around on the ground and weeping in the corners. Inside the old church was stained glass, live music, candlelight. The candles smelled of vanilla. A trust exercise. The therapist picked the woman up and lifted her and carried her around. Her eyes were closed. She had no impulse to open them.

The therapist was not in love with the woman at this point. He thought she was attractive and interesting. Actually, he forgot the whole thing; he had done this exercise with so many others. She was already in love with him, though. Or what she believed love to be at the time. Like so many of my women, it didn't take much for her to fall. Trust is an aphrodisiac.

Inglewood

The woman's friend had a benefit to support the movement work she did with prison inmates. She'd never been so far south on La Brea. Even after living here her whole life. She felt a little ashamed about this. The streets were deserted in the evening. The light had a gray concrete tinge to it. She went up the narrow gallery stairs into the room buzzing with heat and sound. The therapist was there. He told her his favorite piece was a small black and white photograph of some skulls. Then he said, "I went to Auschwitz for a blessing ceremony. People from all over the world came. I took these photographs while I was there and..."

"There were ghosts in the pictures?" the woman said.

"How did you know?" asked the therapist.

The woman didn't know how she knew.

But on their first date he showed her the pictures and there were ghosts in them. Floating over the remains of the ovens.

Less history means less ghosts. There are more and more of them here these days. But not like Auschwitz (thank fucking God). At least I can say that for myself.

Beverly Hills

The woman came here to see the plastic surgeon who had botched her nose job almost ten years ago. She had been too busy before, having children and all.

The surgeon took her nose in his fingertips, squeezed it lightly and said, "I really twisted it to the left, didn't I?"

Well, that's what she heard. In a letter to her later, after her inquiry for help from him, he insisted he never said that. Maybe he said, "It is really twisted to the left, isn't it?

The woman asked what they could do. "I can try to do it again but there may be bad scarring because of how thin-skinned you are," the surgeon said.

"Is there anything else you can do?"

"Kenalog injections. It might take some of the swelling out of the tip."

The woman went home and found herself running to the bathroom to grab the tip of her nose in between playing trains and dress up with her children. She knew she had to do something.

The woman hated Beverly Hills. When her mother was young she lived there. The mother had perfect blond hair and perfect red lips and perfect shoes. But then she divorced her first husband and moved to Laurel Canyon and became a hippie and never went back into Beverly Hills again. So the woman grew up with that prejudice. But she had to go there to see all the doctors she needed. She hadn't been as healthy as her mother was. She needed to pay nice men to tell her she was all right.

She hated Beverly Hills but if you looked at it objectively, you could appreciate it. The streets were still small and charming. There was cheap parking some places. There was a stretch of lovely park. Homes with shade trees and sloping lawns. No sparse, dead grass at the edge of the pavement like in front of the woman's house. All the best stores. Fountains. Tiles. Sparkling things. The woman had to admit she loved sparkling things. She was a secret magpie.

Everyone had pretty hair and surgically enhanced faces. The woman went back and found another doctor who told her that Kenalog injections would make the displaced cartilage in the tip of her nose look much more prominent. Plus, it was steroids, in her face. He told her he could help her. He told her the other doctor had used an old technique of taking cartilage out of the inner nose and trying to rebuild a false squared tip, but that often this slipped over time. He wasn't as handsome or charming as the first doctor. But when the woman closed her eyes and imagined them side by side he was light and the other man was a shadow.

So she had her nose done again. She hadn't gone out with the therapist from dance yet. She had only talked with him, danced with him. But as she was going under she saw him standing at the foot of her bed.

Beverly Hills is a weird place. When she was a kid, the girl remembered a girl she knew named Beverly Hill. She wondered if it was a coincidence. Or an attempt at status. Or sadistic parents.

On their first date, the woman and the therapist went to a gallery opening in Beverly Hills. He knew the artist and many women at the gallery. He hugged them all and told them they looked, "gorgeous." The woman still had bruises from the surgery, like a battered wife. At first the bruises covered most of her face and were bright purple. Her five-year-old daughter said, "They are a pretty color, Mommy," trying not to be afraid, and to make her mother feel better. The therapist was taking aback by the bruises on the woman's cheeks and by how thin she looked. He thought she was anorexic. She told him she had been, in college, she was okay now, only stressed. He said it was his stuff, that it was Auschwitz stuff. She tried not to take his reaction personally.

He showed her the photographs of Auschwitz later that evening. There were actual ghosts in the pictures. The woman wept and he held her in his arms. He said, "You go back and forth between looking so open and so afraid."

"I am," she said. "Open and afraid."

That night, on the streets of Beverly Hills, she had lost her favorite piece of jewelry — an intricately beaded cuff bracelet that her ex-husband had splurged on one Christmas. She wondered if it had jumped from her body, sensing her betrayal. She hoped a homeless person had found it in the night, and not a Beverly Hills housewife who could have easily afforded to purchase it.

Venice

Grace died. She died while the woman was writing this story down for me. She thinks she wrote it but I dictated it to her, you see. Grace died from tumors on her heart, leaving her gentle husband and her tiny, young, bewildered children, and the memorial was on the beach in Venice. Her friends played drums and didgeridoo and danced and wept, stripped off their clothes and plunged into the water. The therapist's ex-girlfriend was there, the one who had broken his heart, the one I can't tell you too much about. Girlfriend. She was naked in the ocean. (I'll tell you this much: too-bright eyes and too-flushed cheeks, pretty, lost, so young.) The therapist was naked too. Grace had introduced them a long time ago. The woman who is writing this story sat alone on the beach watching them. She shivered, watching the man she thought she loved naked in the dark waves with the young, young woman, Girlfriend, who had broken his heart. She felt the spirits of all the unfinished dead yowling through her body. She was possessed.

(I've possessed her, too. She thinks she has her own words but they are all mine.)

The therapist came out of the water, dripping, shivering. He was easy in his publicly naked body, the breadth of his shoulders and chest, his long legs, his penis. The woman wanted to run from him. She wanted to run down the beach away from him, away from me. Summerville. Ojai. Santa Barbara. And on. Healthier. Berkeley. Santa Cruz. Away away.

Instead she held out a towel and wrapped him in it as she would her own children from the bath, and wrapped him in her arms.

This isn't really what happened. It's what she wishes. That's what stories are for, right? A message to the people you have known—this is what I wish I could have been.

I, too, wish I could be different. No smog. No traffic

accidents. Bodies splayed across the windshields of cars. Once I had orange groves and movie studios and ozone. I was a hot young thing. People are still dying for me, but it's not in the same way, you know?

Venice, Later

Once, the therapist and the woman went to the Figtree Café to get some chai lattes before a dinner party. The woman wore an apricot silk velvet dress with shirring at the waist, golden platform ankle-strap shoes that she had envisioned in her mind the day she found them on sale at Shoe Pavilion, and a citrine and pearl triple-strand necklace that she believed had magical powers. The woman and the therapist walked on the boardwalk among the rolling people. Even the rollerblading man with the white turban and the electric guitar was there. The woman had seen him since she was a teenager. He hadn't aged at all. They smelled pot. The woman suddenly wanted some. There were cheap dresses and sunglasses and she wanted those, too. She suddenly wanted everything. And nothing.

They walked across the sand. As soon as their bare feet touched, something happened. The light was pearlized. The woman felt the cool salt on her bare arms. She felt his eyes on her ass, warming her through the thin velvet. His hands and arms were hard, sinewy, brown. He scared the shit out of her sometimes.

They got down to the water and there was an elaborate sand castle, right there, built right in front of them. They hadn't seen it until they came right up to it. It was partly demolished but the outer fortress held. The woman stood inside the sand castle and looked out over the blue-gray luminescence. He put his hard arms her. She had never felt so protected, so safe.

"This should be *de rigueur* when we have kids," he said, meaning the beach.

She couldn't stop laughing. They had been talking about having babies together, if they were a little younger.

He said, "No, I mean have your kids, with us."

She still laughed and laughed. It bubbled through her like the waves foaming onto the sand. She was so happy. So safe. She loved her city. Where else could you find such a sand castle? Such discounted golden shoes? Such an evening? Such a man?

Culver City

It is an afternoon in early fall, the air just starting to chill. The woman and the therapist are lying on her bed after having made love. The woman came all the way, this time, because she touched herself while he was inside of her. After she came she thought about the therapist's ex-girlfriend.

The woman will say softly, "Sometimes I wonder why you haven't introduced us. I mean, it is a little awkward. We see each other all the time at dance and you never introduce us."

"I just don't feel comfortable. I just don't think it is really any of her business."

"And also, how you never want to take one car when we go to the dance place. You always want to meet me."

"I just don't think our relationship is anyone else's business," he will say in a sober, therapist voice.

"Remember how you said she was the love of your life?" the woman will say, feeling as if she is falling and can't stop herself. "That was a little hard for me to hear."

"Well, she was the love of my life. I have never loved anyone that unconditionally, like a parent loves a child. I never even loved my own children that way."

The woman will break up with the man soon after that. Just as she praised me for their relationship in the beginning, now she will blame me for it. She will blame me for Grace's death, too. The UV rays and all. But she will not leave me. She loves me too much. If I do say so myself, I am the love of her life.

Sex and the Spirits

This is a city of glamorous spirits. Quite a few of them are too young, movie-star material. Some utterly heroic. They aren't going to just go quietly. They need to be remembered.

It seems that the spirits leave the woman alone when she is having a relationship with someone. As soon as she stops, they come back.

She went to a meeting for sex and love addicts up in the hills of Malibu. An old, rambling monastery overlooking the sea. She didn't dress in sexy clothes because she had been told to be mindful of what you might provoke at meetings like these. It made her mildly depressed not to be able to wear one of her sheer, sparkled tunics or her high-heeled boots.

There was a man with a baby face and a long-legged dancer's body. His voice was gravelly and slightly sarcastic in tone like the voice of a precocious teenager. He had sharp eyes and a sharp goatee that seemed intended as a distraction from the softness of his face and mouth. He wore a black long-sleeved fitted T-shirt and black jeans and black motorcycle boots and sunglasses so that the woman couldn't see his eyes. She found herself staring fetishistically at the boots, the way the band of metal on the outside of the built-up toe gleamed. (Ever since she was a teenager with spiked hair she had some kind of visceral reaction to boots of this kind. It was a guilty feeling, somewhat masochistic and always sexual. Eventually, after she had slept with too many abusive skinheads, she bought and proudly wore some steel-toed boots of her own.) He sat at her table in the cafeteria where they tried to piece together a vegetarian meal with pasta from the meaty buffet, and peas and hardboiled eggs from the salad bar. He shared some almonds he had brought from home. ("You need protein," he maternally declared.) And she cleared his dishes ("I think you might have to marry me," he told her).

After lunch a group of people from the meeting took a walk down the winding hill, past the canyon ranches and mansions, to the Starbucks. The woman—Angeli, let's call her—walked with the man. The day was chill but gorgeous. As they walked down among the trees toward the ocean, the man's voice changed. It became less loud and sarcastic, softer and more soothing. He took off his sunglasses and his eyes were piercing, obsessively focused but actually quite sad. Angeli told the man about the last relationship she had been in. How the therapist she was dating was still in love with his young ex-girlfriend. How he was haunted by the Holocaust. She told the man in black—let's call him Blackie—about her marriage, how her ex-husband had stopped touching her.

She showed him the pictures of her children in her wallet. (Sometimes she couldn't bear to look at their photographs because they reminded her that every second they were all changing, every second was bringing her closer to a time when she would not be able to see their faces.)

Blackie said, "They're beautiful. Her eyes are exactly like yours."

She laughed. "Most people say, 'They must look like their dad.' Or, 'How did you ever get such gorgeous kids?'"

"People say some weird shit."

She talked about the relationship with the therapist who was still in love with his young ex-girlfriend. The man in black scowled and shook his head at this story. All his senses seemed tuned to her while she spoke. She could tell because he leaned in close, cocking his head, his eyes vampirically dark. He was an actor so he knew how to listen. She liked actors for another reason—they were easy to project onto. They might become, at least temporarily, whoever you wanted them to be. She wanted someone who would listen. Someone kind. Someone hard and soft at the same time. Of course, she had thought that's what she'd found when she met the therapist, too. And he was taking acting lessons, in spite of his successful career. Of course, he was taking acting lessons. Aren't they all? That's why they come to L.A. Even Angeli's ex-husband had moved there to act.

Angeli overheard the man, Blackie, talking to another man later that day. Blackie was saying, "I know what you mean. Alcohol was easy to give up compared to this. This one is hard. I mean, women…"

Angeli decided to ignore this. She had not heard it, after all. She had overheard it, which, she believed, or decided to believe, did not count.

Angeli and Blackie talked some more, in the courtyard by the fountain, among the roses, overlooking the ocean that you could smell in the breeze. The sun glanced off the metal of Blackie's boots and she told him the boots had to go, they were hypnotizing her. He laughed. She said it had been weird for her not to wear her usual clothes to meetings. He asked what she meant.

"You know. I was going to wear my see-through silk shirt with the sequins and my pink suede boots…"

"So no one will get triggered unless you have that on?" he said, smirking slightly, letting his eyes flit over her body for a moment.

"I'm not used to having to dress a certain way," she said. "That's what's cool about being a writer."

They talked about how corny it sounded to say that writing had saved their lives, but also how completely true it was. They talked about how you could use it to give meaning to the worst things in life.

"What is your worst thing?" she asked.

Blackie told her about his father's cancer. She had a feeling, from looking at his eyes, that there had been even worse things.

"But I held him in my arms while he died," Blackie said. "I'm really grateful for that. This program can really suck but it does help you find things to be grateful for."

"My dad had cancer, too," she said. "But I was scared to be in the room while he was dying. I couldn't handle it."

"How old were you?" Blackie asked, scrutinizing her.

"Twenty-one."

"I was forty," Blackie said. "You were a kid."

He told her something else: he told her that one day while his father was lying in the hospital bed, he went outside to smoke a cigarette and was deciding if he should bring his father back with him to Los Angeles or just leave him in the hospital, when a voice distinctly spoke to him.

"Open your heart," the voice said.

Blackie asked for her email so he could let her know about a meeting he was starting at his house. Angeli suddenly remembered why she had come to the retreat. Not to meet men. To heal from men. She told him she couldn't come to the meeting. The whole way home on P.C.H. with the ocean winking its sexy, awe-striking light at her, she regretted this decision. What if the spirits came back?

Shira

On her way back from the retreat, Angeli was thinking about Shira, a young woman she had mentored.

Shira looked like a model, she got straight A's, and she had sold a screenplay at the age of sixteen.

Shira died in a small plane crash in the middle of Los

Angeles when she was only twenty-four years old. For some reason, Angeli was thinking about Shira. How beautiful she was and how smart and how her mother must feel and how Angeli herself would feel if she lost her own daughter. It defied description—that loss. There were no metaphors to give it shape or sense and poetic writing could do that for her with almost anything else. It had done that for Shira.

Her name, Shira, it meant song.

Angeli stopped at the video store because she was depressed and because her children were going to spend the night with their dad and because she didn't want to think about Blackie. If she thought about Blackie she might masturbate and, according to the program she was in, she wasn't supposed to do that for a while, until she healed some more. (She hated that word: masturbation. It was such an ugly word. It sounded harsh and shameful and once she had to say it out loud in a meeting when she was stating the things she couldn't do. It was mortifying to say; not so much because of the act itself but because of the word.) And she didn't want to think about Shira because it was more than sad. It was a tragedy and Shira never liked tragedy. She wrote biting, funny, magical satire with hopeful endings. So Angeli stopped at a Blockbuster in West L.A. and looked for a video but the one she wanted was all out, of course. So she was leaving when the young, blond Hispanic girl behind the counter said, "How about this one?" and handed her a movie and she just took it, not knowing a thing about it. And when she got home and put it on, there was Shira's name on the screen. It was Shira's story that someone else had adapted after her death. But Angeli hadn't heard about it because she and Shira had lost touch in the last few years before the accident. She recognized the character of Shira in the movie and the actress looked just like Shira, except perhaps slightly less beautiful. At the end of the film there was a dedication to Shira Rosen and the dates of her life. 1980-2004. It looked so short when you saw it that way.

So, to Angeli, this was an example of a visitation. Shira was certainly there in the video store and she was certainly there in the living room with the woman who was missing her children who were at their dad's house. And if the Angeli had been having sex, with someone or by herself to a story about Blackie, Shira would not have come.

Not that she didn't want Shira to come. It was just hard, painful. Shira had long blond hair, tanned skin, an infectious smile; she was very tall and wore tank tops with logos on them, very short skirts, high-heeled expensive shoes, and designer sunglasses. She wanted to be a female Fellini. She was so smart and funny and she believed in taking risks and living adventures if you were going to be a writer because how else could you write anything worth reading? Angeli was not nearly this brave. She would never go up in a small plane no matter how exhilarating, no matter how inspirational the view. She had to write about other people's adventures, even sexual ones. Her own weren't worth reading about.

(When Angeli went back to Blockbuster to thank the girl at the counter, she looked at her blankly and recited the special deal they were having in a robotic, fluorescent-light-induced monotone, with no recognition of having delivered Shira's movie into Angeli's hands.)

Angeli managed not to email Blackie, though they had exchanged addresses and he wrote her once, inviting her to the meeting at his house again. She didn't respond but she did look him up online, of course. After all, she had identified herself as a sex and love addict, so what do you expect? She discovered that he was quite a successful actor and had also directed two films. It looked like a couple of the films he had been in were un-rated and had sexual themes. She wondered if they were porn and what it would be like to have sex with a porn actor. She couldn't imagine being with someone who liked to fuck more than she did or who could keep it going long enough. She had just about given up on the possibility of ever finding this, especially after being told by the last man she had dated that she was too wet all the time, that it was difficult for him to come with all that lubrication. She wondered if someone like Blackie would mind if she were wet or if she rubbed herself with the knuckle of her middle finger while he was inside of her. He seemed like the type of man who wouldn't mind, who might actually appreciate it. In fact, she might not need to do this to herself—he might know how to do it for her. Or, better yet, he might know how to find that elusive star-shooting spot inside of her that only one man, her ex-husband, had accidentally found once when, engorged with the desire to get pregnant, she conceived her first child. She wondered what kind of body Blackie must have to be in porn. His head shot on line made him look sexier and more brooding and more dangerous and more handsome than he did in real life. In real life he seemed vulnerable and sad and that made her like him even more.

So she didn't email Blackie or even touch herself. And then she had another visitation.

Adam

When she was pregnant with her son, four years before, Angeli hired a labor coach. She asked the labor coach if she was also available as a doula, to help with the birth. The labor coach said no, she had given that up a long time ago and though she liked Angeli, she couldn't help her. Angeli kept asking the labor coach; for some reason she felt it was essential to have this woman at her side when she gave birth to her son. Finally, the labor coach agreed. "Because I like you and because your due date is a week before my son's birthday." It also turned out that the name Angeli and her husband had chosen for their baby was the name of the labor coach's son.

Angeli was a week late giving birth. She went to visit the

labor coach at her home. The woman showed her a photograph of a young man striding confidently down an airport runway with an indigenous woman at his side.

"That's my son, Adam. The one whose birthday is next week. Isn't he handsome? He works in South America trying to preserve the rain forests. He has a great fiancé here who is already like my daughter."

Angeli couldn't stop thinking about Adam. She thought about him when she went into labor with her son. She stared into his mother's eyes when the pain peaked so high it lifted her from the bed. She was levitating with pain but Adam's mother kept her grounded, kept her from leaving her body entirely.

When Angeli's son was finally out and in her arms she kissed his damp, downy head, she whispered how she loved him. Then she turned to Adam's mother and said, "How was your son's birthday? Didn't you say it was this week?"

"It's today," Adam's mother said. Something looked wrong in her face and Angeli asked, "What? What is it?"

And Adam's mother said, "It's a sad story. You don't want to hear it today."

"Oh yes, I do," Angeli said. "You have to tell me. Please."

So as Angeli's new baby discovered how to make milk come out of her body for the first time, Adam's mother told her that Adam had died two years ago. He had been slain in Columbia by a rebel group that believed he was working against them, for the U.S. government. And Angeli was nursing her newborn son who shared Adam's name and birthday when she heard this news.

Adam's mother gave Angeli a video about him and she stayed up all night nursing her son by the soft light of a lamp in the shape of a globe, and they watched Adam's video again and again. It seemed to her that Adam looked a little like a combination of her and her handsome then-husband.

"Adam," she said aloud, while her baby sucked milk out of

her body like he was trying to make her disappear inside of him. She would have easily complied if she could.

Angeli wanted to put her baby down in his bed next to his sister's and climb on top of her husband and jam their bodies together until she levitated but she knew he would have rolled over and then she really would have been alone.

This is how Adam visited Angeli almost four years later, after her divorce: Angeli's girlfriend came over with a video about meditation. This friend had lost her forty-five-year-old husband to cancer a year before. When Angeli asked her girlfriend how she had survived this, she said it was through meditation. Angeli had tried to meditate before but she never could until her friend mentioned it. It was as if a spell was broken. And every day after that conversation Angeli got up at five in the morning, lit a candle and sat while her children slept. The girlfriend kept suggesting ways to enhance the meditation and that was what the video was. On the video there was an interview with a young woman who said that she had found meditation after her boyfriend had been killed in Columbia. And Angeli said to her girlfriend, "Adam! She's talking about Adam!" And, yes, it was Adam and this was his fiancée. They had come into Angeli's living room. She had to turn off the video and light a candle and tell the story to her friend. And then she cried and wished she could just numb herself with a good fuck so she didn't have to think about dead people anymore.

The spirits of this city like to come via film. That shouldn't surprise you.

Adam reached Angeli one more time. She wrote a short story about him, and a mother at her children's pre-school read it and said, "That sounds like the boyfriend of someone I know. His name was Adam."

Tears jumped into Angeli's eyes of their own volition and she said, "That is Adam."

"I'm really good friends with his girlfriend," this other

mother said. "I'll introduce you if you'd like."

So at a children's birthday party among the cake gooey with frosting and the balloons twisted into animals and the bouncy-house in the shape of a giant red dog, Angeli was introduced to Adam's girlfriend, Anna. Her hair was in dark ringlets just like his, and she had the same glowing brown skin and big dark eyes but her features were tiny and delicate and her body was willowy and light. Angeli couldn't help herself; she told Anna the whole story of Adam's mother and the birth of her son and Anna started to cry. Angeli felt like a complete ass and apologized but Anna said, "It happens all the time. This is my life. He touched so many people. It's okay. Thank you for telling me." But Angeli wished that the spirits would leave her alone so that she could spend a birthday party talking about food allergies and excessive consumerism and how big the children were getting, like everybody else.

Grace

These are the stories of two of the spirits. Angeli was afraid that, without sex, there would be more and more of them. One she expected was Grace, a dancer, a friend of the therapist she had dated. Grace had died of melanoma, leaving her husband and young twins behind. Angeli didn't know Grace but she had seen her dance in a way that made everyone in the room slow down to watch her. She had seen the faces of Grace's children — the wispy hair, blond like their mother's, and the forlorn eyes. She had seen Grace's husband, Gerald, wandering around a party with his son bobbing high on his broad but recently bony shoulders and his daughter holding his hand, a few weeks after Grace's death. Mia, the ex-girlfriend of the therapist Angeli had dated, stopped Gerald, took his hands in hers, looked into his lost face and kissed him on the mouth but he backed away from her after that.

Angeli wasn't sure she could handle Grace's spirit. She was a mom, after all. She had to be present, grounded. She couldn't be talking to spirits, no matter how beautiful or tragic they were, how dear to her or to the loved ones they had left.

Angeli had her hair blow-dried at a salon and put on makeup. She put on strands of fake fresh water pearls and a silk camisole and an embroidered silk coat and her tightest blue jeans and patent leather platforms. Then she got in her car and drove along the misty coast past the constellation of the Ferris wheel and up into Topanga Canyon, a place to which spirits, as well as artists and hipsters and hippies, were partial.

Blackie was at the party. She was so nervous that she only said a quick hello and walked away, waiting for him to come up to her if he wanted to. He seemed to be ignoring her and when she left the warm room with the fireplace and the music, the night in the canyon felt especially cold and the stars looked especially harsh and the murmur of the trees was like ghosts. She went home and masturbated to ward off the spirits, realizing that in some ways she had used men to avoid slipping into that other world. Shira's world, Adam's world, Grace's world.

After a yoga class, sweaty and with no makeup on, Angeli went to a café in Santa Monica for a green tea rice milk and tapioca pearl boba and ran into the therapist she had dated. He looked a lot older than when she had last seen him. He said, "A month after you broke up with me, my father died. And a month after that, I had a stroke. But I've been processing it and I forgive you. I've changed my life. I gave up my practice and I started taking more acting improv classes. Mia's in there and we've healed our relationship."

Mia was the therapist's young ex-girlfriend, the one he would never introduce to Angeli, the one who was, in part, the reason for their break up.

"I'm glad you're okay," Angeli said. Suddenly the boba balls tasted cloying and gummy.

That night she got an email from Blackie. It said, "Are you ignoring me? Because it seemed at the party as if you were ignoring me. And I really think you are a nice person. And you also looked really pretty."

"I thought you were ignoring me!" she wrote back.

Angeli changed her mind and went over to Blackie's house for the meeting. He had a big Spanish house with lots of glass overlooking the Hollywood hills. There was almost no furniture and really bad art on the walls. A lurid faux 1800's battle scene in a gaudy gold frame and a tepid landscape and a lousy Picasso imitation.

"Isn't the art hideous?" Blackie chuckled.

Angeli didn't know what to say.

"I was at an auction and the woman next to me told me to bid on it so I did. I'm such a sex and love addict!"

"You bought it because she told you to?"

"I'm a sex and love addict!" Blackie said. "What do you want?"

He had a cat named Baby he had found at his doorstep. He had a violin that he actually played. He had posters of *La Strada* and *La Dolce Vida* on the wall beside the hideous art. He had shelves full of acting books and classic novels. There was a picture of him as a teenager with wild black curls, that brooding baby face and the sad eyes of a mature man.

Blackie had three by five cards pasted on the wall above his desk for the screenplay he was writing. The title was *Sex and the Spirits*. Angeli laughed and said, "That could be my life story."

"It's mine," Blackie said matter-of-factly.

At the meeting she shared: "I keep slipping in my program. My bottom lines feel pretty strict. I mean I have biological responses and I sometimes break my bottom lines. But at least I'm not getting involved with anyone. I mean, I'm alone and meditating and taking care of my kids and going to meetings and I guess I'm doing okay."

Blackie raised his hand and she called on him. He squinted across the room at her as if something was hurting him. She had learned this was just the way he looked when he was concentrating hard.

"I hired this personal assistant. This really young woman and she was helping me market. She took this bunch of broccoli and started walking down the aisle with it like a bouquet and humming "Here Comes the Bride." And then I realized that I was falling for her. She was totally unavailable and inappropriate and I had to fire her. But at least I didn't have to get into anything the way I would have in the past.

She was the last one to leave. "Can I make you something to eat?" he asked. Magic words, she thought, coming from a man.

He stir-fried some tofu with ginger and garlic and cooked brown rice and she made the salad with the organic lettuce, pomegranate seeds and persimmons she found in his refrigerator. They made the dressing together — extra virgin olive oil, raspberry vinegar, garlic, a pinch of salt, a squirt of lime. Neither drank alcohol anymore so they had sparkling grapefruit in fluted champagne glasses. Blackie lit a fire in the fireplace and they sat on the black leather couch and ate their food in large natural ceramic bowls. It was hard for her to resist a man who cooked for her and played the violin and wrote screenplays and liked Fellini. Also took in strays. Baby came and rubbed against her feet.

"She likes you," Blackie said. "She usually won't come out when I have guests."

Angeli stroked Baby's back in the overly sensual way she tended to pet animals when in the close proximity of a man she wanted to fuck. "I like her," she said. Then she said, "I'm not supposed to even be here. I'm not supposed to hang out with men who trigger me."

"So I trigger you," Blackie said.

"Yes. And I'm not supposed to even tell you that because

supposedly it might trigger you."

"Then why are you here?"

"I am trying to avoid the spirits," she said.

Francisco

Angeli told Blackie a story of another visitation about ten years before, right after her father had died of cancer. She was in Joshua Tree, visiting her best friend, Francisco who moved out there because he had AIDS and he needed to get away from the city. So she went to see Francisco, whom she loved but who would never have sex with her, and she was sitting outside of his adobe house in the late afternoon sun. The wind swept over the desert and something was crackling and dancing at her fingertips. She saw it was a piece of crumpled paper and she picked it up and unfolded it. The paper was a letter to her from her father. He had written it a year before but she had lost it. And somehow it had followed her out here and turned up in her hand. It told her how we are all made of stars, how some of us came from the same star and will continue to find each other again and again. That night, Angeli and Francisco lay on their backs on the roof of his adobe and watched stars careening across the sky. Francisco strummed his guitar and made up a song about what had happened and sang it to her.

After Angeli had given birth to her second child, Francisco died. Angeli and her children drove out to the desert for his funeral. It was a full moon; Francisco was a self-proclaimed lunatic, meaning moon-man and so, of course, it was full, as if he had winkingly arranged it. Angeli felt so distant from herself that she couldn't cry. She just held her children in her arms and listened to Francisco's friends playing their guitars and telling stories about him — how he always wrote songs for them, how he always made them strong cups of coffee and called them angel, how his home was always open to everyone, how more stars seemed to shoot across the sky above his roof than anywhere else--and watched them putting flowers on an altar. And then Francisco's father, who had survived two heart attacks, got up and walked to the altar and put something down there. Angeli saw it was Francisco's desert boots, the ones he always wore. This is what finally brought her back into herself so that she could cry.

Angeli kept waiting for a visitation from Francisco but it never came. He was different from the others—Shira and Adam and even from her father. He was done with this world. He hadn't had a boyfriend for years, since he'd been diagnosed with the disease. Some people said he seemed like a celestial being. His brown skin so translucent and a radiance around his bleach-blond head. He didn't need to come to visit again, although, sometimes, Angeli would smell the natural oil he wore, an intoxicating vanilla, coming out of nowhere, or hear his voice in her mind as if he were whispering in her ear.

She and Blackie did not sleep together. Or, rather, they slept together but they did not have sex. Blackie had a brand new, plastic wrapped toothbrush for her to have and a men's pajama shirt for her to borrow. He wore the matching pajama pants and she kept her underwear on. He lit some sage green candles. They lay beside each other on Blackie's big black lacquer frame bed. Baby slept against Angeli's belly, thrumming.

Grace was standing in the wings, omniscient as these spirits are, watching the blank black glass of the big screen TV on the wall, waiting for her close up.

Apocalypsex

Awake

Angeli did not really notice Mateus for a long time, even though their sons attended the same pre-school. He did not notice her either. First of all, they were married to other people. Besides this, Angeli and Mateus were both asleep. Sometimes it takes grief to wake someone up. But it must be grief mixed with hope, otherwise the grief will put you to sleep forever.

It was their children who were the hope.

Create

As an artist you have to make things happen. You have to. That was what creation was, right? It was how Angeli had survived since she was a teenager. But mostly she did it by herself. And on the page.

She wrote about kissing the back of his neck where the black hair formed tight curls like thick little fists. Once, at his son's fourth birthday party, she had ridden in the tiny train car behind Mateus and felt as fascinated with the tightness and blackness of the curls on his nape as perhaps her son and his felt about trains going around and around a track that did not end. Transfixed.

She wrote about how he would take off his T-shirt and her hands would explore the slope of his shoulders, the warmth of his abdomen. Once, at the boys' pre-school, he had stretched, absently, languidly, showing off the pattern of hair around his navel, his fingers grazing himself there and she had imagined that he was doing this for her. On a dizzily hot summer day they had gone swimming and she had seen the power of his ass and the solid, sensual shape of his pecs, both usually hidden beneath baggy clothes, and he had seen her body stretched out at the edge of the pool, on the hot pavement that left red marks later, nearly naked in a black bikini with a large silver ring between her breasts and at her left hip.

She wrote about undressing for him. Before her showers now, she practiced. Standing with her back to the mirror, glancing over her shoulder. First her jeans came off, slowly slithering over her hips. He'd see the roundness of her ass, the dimples in her lower back. Then she'd pull off her shirt, skillfully unhook her bra, let it fall way. Her hands would cup her breasts. They had nursed two babies, simultaneously, but they were still suckable, sensitive. Her back still to him, she'd yank her modest panties up into a thong. She'd wiggle out of them, step out of them, bending down so he might glimpse the dark, glistening space between her thighs. Then turn to him, swollen by this time, her body slippery with desire. And she imagined how he would envelop her nakedness then, erasing that feeling of exposure and vulnerability as he carried her onto the bed. She had seen that bed when she went over to pick her son up from a play date. It was crazy hot but the apartment was air-conditioned so she stopped sweating for the first time that day. The boys were hiding under the red comforter and the gauzy drapes at the window were blowing slightly in the blasts of cool air. She guiltily tried to see what books and DVDs were beside his bed. She kept the image of his bedroom in her mind, to use that night when she touched herself, thinking of him. He had seen her bed, too. His eyes had lingered on it for a second; it was a big bed with roses and her tight blue jeans with the rhinestone trim were spread out there and he had looked at them and at it in that fierce but swiftly secretive way he had, almost too quick for her to catch.

She wrote about getting down on her knees, offering herself to him any way he wanted. *I'll strip for you, go down on you, kiss every part of you, do backbends and splits for you, let you put every part of you into every orifice of me.* Here she was, trying to create it again. By herself. She finished the story. It felt too personal, too exposing for both of them. If he never touches me, she thought, if we never get closer, I'll have this story. I'll disguise his character and maybe I'll publish it. That will have to be enough. But if he comes to me, I will give this story only to him.

And then he took her picture. She had called him in a panic, needing something right away for an online magazine article someone was doing about her. She hated to be photographed. The Native American concept that a picture could steal your soul felt dangerously true. Unless it was by someone who could momentarily borrow your soul, connect to it and return it to you, perhaps stronger, perhaps nurtured. He said, "I photograph people the way I see them." In the photograph it looked like she wore a crown of the purple agapanthus flowers that grew in the background. All the best things she felt inside filled her face in that picture. All the wonderment and delight at her children, all the pain-obliterating joy of dancing, all the anticipation of his kisses. In her eyes was his reflection, in her smile was her crush—radiant, expansive, unabashed.

He asked her to see a movie with him, a grown-up movie without the kids. She imagined he would act as if they weren't really going out on a date, just hanging out, not a date. But she had her hair blown out and bought a new dress—white, sweet, not too sexy, but a halter without a bra, which she never wore. Her children lay on their bellies on the floor of the dressing room, gazing up. Her son said, dreamily, "You look so pretty,

Mommy." Her daughter said, gravely. "Oh yes. But why do you need that? Are you going on a date with a *boy?*" Angeli even got a bikini wax on the hottest day ever recorded in California. The wax blistering on the tender skin, the rip of the strip.

She almost ran out the door when he got there. He stopped her. His voice could be soft, intended only for one. He said, "Not so fast. I have something for you." His eyes could be warm as chocolate melting in a pot over a blue gas flame. Behind his back were flowers chosen in the colors she wore—white daisies and pink and white freesia and large white spiky chrysanthemums wrapped tenderly in white netting to keep their petals fresh and safe.

She hadn't expected this. It made her hands shake so much she could hardly get the flowers into water. "I'm so nervous," she said.

"The flowers are so you don't feel nervous."

"They make me more nervous," she said. "I love them."

Later, after the movie, they sat in the car for a moment. She said, "It's so weird. I feel like I know you so well and not at all."

"I know exactly what you mean," he said.

She said, "I don't know what to do now."

"Well, you have to let me in to help you with those flowers." He arranged them for her. She rolled the chrysanthemum netting up her leg like a stocking and stuck a few of the stray broken freesia in the black hair that curled on either side of his head like tiny horns.

She was afraid to touch him. Once, when their arms had brushed at a kid's play at the library, just the hairs on their arms, she had felt the electricity of him jolt through her body. (It was a play about the Mayans. When it was over, he had turned to her and whispered, "According to the Mayan calendar, the world is supposed to end six years from now. 2012." Because of the way he said it—he was a Scorpio—it sounded somehow erotic and not apocalyptic. Later, he clarified, "I don't believe it will end *per se*, just end as we know it, be better.) What would happen when he touched more of her? "You might blow my mind," she said. She was afraid that if she undressed for him entirely, let him into her, that she wouldn't be able to let him leave that night, go back to his apartment. She'd heard somewhere that when women exercised, to prevent bone loss, they should do something called "shock their bones." It would be like that. Bone shock. Blood shock. Love shock. So they rolled around on the floor, mostly clothed, telling each other things about their pasts, their bodies. She was surprised at his candor, at his poetry. She felt him through his blue jeans, so hard and imperative. It would have been too much, how could she let go of his lithe warm skateboarder body, let him go home if she let him inside her? He said, "I can wait now. I'm not in a rush. Now that I know this is going to happen." Then he left.

He gave her music. It was like all of the loss and desire of her entire life was in those songs. It was like a blood transfusion for congested, oxidized blood. It was like her teenage self woke from the years of sleeping and danced out of the glass coffin. The music created more pictures in her mind. Pictures of what they would do to each other, song by song. They would roll around, still clothed, until he pulled off her jeans and she felt the tough fabric melting into softness and heat. He would bend her into different positions and she would reveal the parts of herself to him. His hands would be in her panties and his thumbs thickly stroking, finding all the nerve endings. They would tug on each other's hair and she would cry from the gorgeous force of him. Falling through into another universe while his music played. The music that told her secrets about him he couldn't have said any other way.

She emailed him to thank him for the CD. She told him she was ovulating and it was August and she always got pregnant in August. He said, "I can't wait anymore."

She went over to his house.

It was not her alone this time creating.

Once he had said to her "I have this belief, that what we create, that becomes our reality. We just have to keep our minds open and see it to believe it."

She did not tell him that just before she met him she had finally taken the time to write down the characteristics she was searching for in a man. He matched all of them exactly.

A Better Place

When she got back home after making love to Mateus for the first time, Angeli's Springer Spaniel was splayed out on the floor whimpering. She tried to help him stand and he kept slipping back down. For the rest of the night she carried him in and out of the house to pee. In the morning she called the vet.

"Usually when people finally make this call, it's time," the vet said.

She knew this was true. For the past few weeks, things like this would happen, every so often, and then her dog would be all right again. But he had never been completely unable to stand.

Angeli's children came over to say good-bye to their doggy.

"Where is he going?" they asked.

"He's going to die," she said.

"When will he be back?"

"He's not coming back."

"Where will he go?"

"He will be somewhere where he won't have a hurt body anymore. His spirit will run free, like when he was a puppy."

"Is that dog heaven?" they asked.

"Yes, we can call it dog heaven."

They made pictures for him where his long, curly ears were wings, transporting him through puffy blue and pink watercolor clouds. They strung plastic flower beads on cord to put around his neck. They helped give him a bath in lavender soap to remove the excrement that was on his fur. Then they kissed him good-bye and their father took them away.

When they left, Angeli called Mateus.

She said, "I don't know if this is okay to ask, but I know you'll just tell me if it doesn't work for you but I have to put my dog to sleep and I really need some male energy."

He came over right away. He sat next to her while the vet sedated her beloved, beautiful old Springer Spaniel who was wearing the necklace of plastic flowers made by the children, and then gave the dog a lethal injection. She held her dog's head in her hands and gazed into his eyes and wept and sobbed. It was the only time Mateus had seen her cry.

The vet said, "Maybe you don't want to watch this part." He had some plastic sheets in his hands.

Angeli took Mateus by the hand and led him into her bedroom.

He said, "I don't know exactly where we go but it is to a better place." For some reason she believed him. "I'm not afraid of death," he said. "We just go on. And we find the spirits of the people we loved. So there really isn't any reason to be afraid."

Superhero

On their next date he said he was going to take her somewhere to surprise her. They drove along P.C.H. as the sun was setting. There was a weird, acidic light. Traffic slowed. They heard sirens and saw police cars. A vehicle was flipped over at the side of the road and there was a body on a stretcher, the bare, bloodied feet exposed. A police helicopter landed in billows of smoke. *The end of the world*, she thought.

They were trapped in traffic like that for what felt like a long time. If she were alone, or, especially, with her children, she would have panicked but she just watched his face. His expression didn't change. And she was strangely calm. But when they escaped the jam and turned up into Topanga, she sighed.

"Hell to heaven," she said.

"It gets better."

They walked down the brick steps into the enclosed patio overhung with trees. There were rose petals in the fountain and twinkle lights strung everywhere. This was where Angeli had been married, right here on this patio. For some reason, she could not bring herself to tell Mateus this (or that she had shivered with a supernatural chill and gagged back giggles through most of the ceremony). She just said it was her favorite restaurant.

He said, "I thought you would like it."

There were no ghosts of her wedding there, only Angeli, in a black dress instead of white, and Mateus in a suit made by a skateboard company, a faded T-shirt and a black bandana over his curls.

They sat at a small table overlooking the dry creek bed. The table was hypnotizing her with candlelight shining on white wine and the narcissus flowers in glass. He sat across from her wearing the gray jacket with zipper pockets and an embroidered logo. It was so cool it made her want to fuck him then and there.

They were talking about the superhero exhibit they had taken their sons to and she hadn't been fully listening to him because of the candlelight and his suit. Then she heard him say, "I always thought it would be cool to just be able to heal someone with your hands. That is the real superpower."

He zapped her forehead with his broad, flat fingers. He was smiling but his smooth voice had a melancholy crack. He had broken his wrist skateboarding and there was a large knobby bone that protruded there; she stroked it before they both got too self-conscious and she let go.

She thought, *Sometimes it feels like we can see inside each other.*

She wondered if he was thinking of the people he loved and couldn't save. His best friend who had committed suicide, his ex-wife who had left him suddenly with no explanation. She wanted to tell him, "You know they had to want it, too; to be saved." She wanted to say, "Tell me, my friend, just now lover, do you know this: That you have already healed me too many times to count. It just takes a burnished glance from under those eyebrows. Arms girding my body and the generous impact of your lips. Not to mention (like ascending from the bloody, smoky highway into the canyon garden), the relief of penetration."

I will inject figs with milk and honey/Call the blackbirds to the window (two for joy)/Write our name in snail track silver on polished river rocks/Put orchids between my legs/Are you willing?/Sometimes receiving is heroic, too

2012

On their next date, they went to see a movie in Pasadena. On the way there she told him she needed to travel, get out of L.A.

"You are!," he said. "Pasadena!"

She laughed. She meant Brazil. She meant Peru. She meant Bali, Tibet, India. He had been insistent on going to this movie and Pasadena was the only place it was playing. There was something old and still about Pasadena. Darker and staid. Old stone, less neon.

On the freeway, she said, "I want to start a magazine with you. Because of that suit you bought."

After the suit made her want to fuck him, it made her want to start a magazine with him. He had been the editor-in-chief of a Brazilian skateboarding magazine when he was twenty-four years old. He always said "editor-in-chief" when he referred to it. So she wanted to start a magazine with him about board sports and poetry and fashion and music, about change and transition and transcendence and the things that took you to the next place. On the way to Pasadena she told him the name she had come up with: "2012."

"So, it's all about transition," he said.

The movie was about recognizing and reading the signs that are around us everyday and appreciating their beauty and wisdom. The ideas in the movie, like the suit, made her want to fuck him and start a magazine with him.

On the way home there was a detour that lead them right up to a brick wall. He stopped at the stop sign, about to turn left to get on the freeway. She started screaming.

He asked calmly, "What?" It was hard to ruffle his feathers. She loved that about him but it also drove her crazy sometimes; sometimes she wanted to just mess him up for the hell of it. When he came, though, he hollered as loudly as she did.

She wasn't thinking about coming now, though. She was jumping around in her seat and pointing and yes, yelling as if she were coming.

On the wall in front of them someone had written some graffiti. Four times, the same message.

2012   2012   2012   2012

And then: "The end is near" and an infinity symbol.

"What the fuck. Oh my God!"

He leaned back calmly in the driver's seat. "I rest my case," he said. "I prove my point."

Signs were everywhere; yes, they were.

She laughed. She said. "We're so crazy. We're all excited, or, I'm excited and you're all like cool, cool, because we saw this sign that says the world is going to end. Let's just go home and celebrate and have sex!"

He said, "That sounds like a good idea. But the world isn't going to end. It's just going to change."

They went home and had end-of-the-world sex anyway.

She decided she would write about making love with him

now. It was too much for her to contain. Her therapist had told her not to share so much with people but she couldn't help it. That was what she did, who she was, a compulsively confessional writer. How embarrassing but the truth.

Star Babies

Every time Angeli and Mateus were together was completely different from the last. It began with the clothes she wore. She planned her outfits carefully, thinking about how they would come off. One night it was black platform shoes, a black dress with a garter belt and black stockings. One night a pair of tight jeans tucked into high boots and a sheer silk blouse. Usually he removed everything for her, or almost everything; he liked to leave one piece of her clothing on—a different one each time. Once she undressed for him, while he was still fully clothed and sat in his lap, the roughness of his jeans between her thighs making her feel more naked.

Sometimes he was forceful and quick and sometimes he was slower and more tender, kissing her mouth for a longer time and rubbing her gently with his fingers until she was just about to come. But he always kissed her, he almost always made sure to be the one to unhook her bra, he always sucked her nipples and sighed at her breasts and he always flipped her over at least once and looked at her ass and pulled off her panties. She almost always bled. This was probably because she was aging and her uterine lining was thinning, but it felt more like her body trying to express its passion in as many ways as possible. He found different ways to enter her but she always writhed and cried out.

The night after they saw the signs she said, "If I weren't on these anti-depressants, I'd cry through this all the time."

And he said, "The worst thing is when you have to cry and you try not to cry. That's the hardest thing. It's better to just cry."

"Before I was on medication that happened to me all the time when I was reading bedtime stories to my children," she said. "I'd be choking back the tears every night."

"It's better to cry," he said.

She took off the glass goddess she wore around her neck.

"Why are you taking her off?" he asked.

"Because she is a fertility goddess. I mean look at her!"

"So?" he said.

"No, no, no fertility goddesses. You don't understand. You don't..." She buried her face in his armpit. He had a warm, slightly fleshy, strong chest, a big chest for a giraffe-sized heart. (At their sons' pre-school, a woman had come in to talk about non-violent parenting. She had said, "You are either a giraffe or a jackal. A giraffe's heart is the biggest organ in its body; the jackal is all stomach.")

"I understand," he said. "I think I do. I know more about you than you think. I know things about you and you don't even have to say them. You don't have to say anything unless you want to."

Did he know that she and her ex-husband had stopped sleeping together for years? That she had thought she was in love with a sixty-year-old therapist who, while he was with her, continually referred to his thirty-year-old ex-girlfriend as "the love of my life." That Blackie had never called her again. Did Mateus know that she already loved his son with such ferocity that she felt she had to hide it, so as not to upset her own boy or the boy's mother? Did Mateus know how much she wanted to make babies with him? That she probably couldn't?

She had been diagnosed with bone loss and anxiety and depression and she had to take so many medications and supplements and she could never have another baby while she was taking them. Plus she was going to be forty-four. But she looked up Portuguese names on the Internet, carefully erasing her tracks as if she were looking up porn. Mirari meant miracle;

Yelena, light, Izabel with a z was gift of god. They would have a baby with large dark eyes and dark curly hair and sensitive fingers and toes, long limbs, a sweet, sweet heart. Probably a girl. Angeli thought. And he was such a good daddy. Patient and kind but firm. He knew himself and he taught that just by his presence. It made her want to have babies with him when he danced with her daughter, took her son on the roller coaster, kissed his own son and watched the boy with so much love that she felt a stab in her solar plexus like her heart seizing up.

To make things worse, Mateus had even told her about "star children," the ones who were being born now, more and more frequently, with their larger heads and wisdom, their food sensitivities and their tendency to say things like, "I want to go home," when supposedly they were already there.

The Opening

When she was in her twenties, Angeli had a boyfriend whom she loved in a way she had never experienced loving anyone before. When she held him, the miracle of his soul's residence in his particular lean, graceful body was apparent to her. She could understand the way his soul manifested itself in the cells of his body. At this time, Angeli had wanted to write a book that was about two people who loved each other. That was all the book would be about. She had no idea how to go about this, or how it would keep anyone's attention but she knew the book was inside her and that one day it would come out, just as she had always felt her children inside of her.

Angeli and the boyfriend broke up suddenly one night, hours after making love and talking about the babies they wanted to have together. Mateus was the first man since then who made Angeli experience that cellular, soulful feeling. And she still wanted to write the book about the two people.

She wondered when would she be able to tell Mateus, "I

love you. Thank God for you. Thank Goddess for you. Thank you for arriving. I have been waiting, just surviving. You have been the reason for my tasks and my loss. You have been the reason for my tests and my grieving. You are like my children; always inside of me, innate, born with me, and therefore it was just short of unbearable to be without you."

Maybe she would never have to; maybe he just knew. When would she know what he was feeling? Maybe she did.

Or maybe these feelings had nothing to do with him. Maybe they were just her longing speaking. Maybe someday she would look back at what she had written bitterly and think, that was all projection, like with the therapist. I never loved him that much. I just wanted to love someone that much.

When she had these thoughts, she felt her chest closing up like a flower or a fist. There was an actual hardening there, in the center of her chest. Who did it harm but herself? she wondered.

Angeli had once been stopped for a siren at a street corner, her children in the car, when a man at a bus stop yelled at her, "Move your fuckin' ass on!" She saw he wore a headset and did not hear the oncoming fire truck. Before she could control herself, she flipped him off and screamed at him.

The next day she was dropping her children off at their father's house when one of his magazines caught her eye. In it was an article by a Buddhist monk, which said that if we respond to pain by closing our hearts, we are only continuing the cycle of pain. An inmate explained why he did not react to mistreatment by guards in the prison by saying that he did not want the man to go home and beat his children, and that, or something like it, is what would occur if he reacted.

Mateus came over one night with a DVD.

"It just jumped out at me," he said.

It was the movie based on Shira's story. Angeli had never told Mateus about any of the spirits. When he handed her the movie, she started saying "Oh my God" over and over again until he made her sit down in a small, flickering pool of candlelight and tell him what was wrong.

"You did it again," she said. Then she told him all about the spirits, about Shira and Adam and Francisco and her father, but not about Grace for some reason; she didn't really know why. Mateus's eyes were full of sorrow and also light. They watched the movie together; they read Shira's name and the dates that framed her life on the screen at the end of the movie. She was there with them, Angeli was sure.

Mateus kissed her forcefully on the lips until she couldn't tell whose breath belonged to whom.

"Speak to me in Portuguese," she said.

"It's such a cliché," he laughed. His eyes were twinkling now.

"Please."

He whispered in the language she did not understand. There were no hard sounds at all. The words spilled out of his mouth onto her body. Slowly, he lifted the pink silk fabric of her camisole and kissed her abdomen, the mysterious words like cool water on her heated flesh. Carefully, he unhooked her black lace bra with the pink roses. She could tell he was proud of how easily he could undress her, how skilled he was with hooks and eyes, buttons and zippers and snaps. He was still speaking in Portuguese, the silken, milky, silky, milken, lilting, throaty, lilty, throaten language. It was his mother tongue, the language he had spoken as a child. A different part of him emerged when he spoke this. He put his big lips on her nipples while his hands reached up the leg of her shorts and inside her panties with the roses. He rubbed her; she writhed under his fingers. Then he turned her over and slid the jeans and then the underpants down over her hips, over her legs, to the ground. He spread her legs apart and unbuckled his belt and put himself inside her mouth. Her throat relaxed and she took more and more of him into her. He moaned and pulled away and kissed her. He was always so poised, even in the hottest moments. He always took out the condom, unrolled it, slid it so easily onto his hardness. She was a puddle by then. She could hardly move. She wished she had a language he didn't understand. Then she would tell him of his beauty, that she loved him and wanted his child. But she had no language of secrets so she only moaned, and when he put himself inside her, she cried.

After, they couldn't sleep. They lay awake tossing and talking, sweating on the sheets.

"It's too much," she said. "You stimulate me too much. We have to find some kind of project to sublimate all this energy or I'm going to want to have your child."

He laughed. And then they got up out of bed and took photographs of orbs.

"What are orbs?" she had asked him.

"Like… spirits. They only show up on the camera. They're drawn out when two people with the right energies come together and make love. I'm trying to document this. Do you want to try? I think different people can perceive them differently and it will show up on the film."

The pictures, developed, showed strange shapes, lights. The colors were muted, swirling, numinous like the clouds in her children's pictures for their dying dog, but shining.

She didn't want to avoid the spirits anymore. When she was with Mateus she wanted them to come to her. Shira and Adam and Francisco and her father and all the others. She wanted to understand what they had to tell her. Death did not seem fearsome when she was with Mateus. She was aware of the steadfastness of the soul and the connections the soul makes with other souls.

One night they got high. He was reclining on the floor and the twinkle lights made the air hazy with glow and there were some sweet-smelling flowers in a glass jar. He was telling her about quantum physics and she was trying to understand him but she didn't quite. But his voice was mesmerizing her, and his long body, spread out on the floor in his T-shirt that said "2012" encased in an infinity sign and his baggy pants and his socks.

"You are so adorable," she said. "I can't fucking stand it how adorable you are." This was said only because she was high; otherwise she would have been too shy. As soon as she said it, he grabbed her and rolled her in his arms. An old Joni Mitchell song sent through her mind, *"roll her in his arms and give his seed to her..."* It was a song about a boy who turned into a statue or a statue who turned into a boy, she couldn't remember which. Angeli and Mateus's bodies rolled over some loose petals and the room smelled of crushed flowers and beeswax.

"I'm not afraid of the spirits," she said. "I want to hear what they have to say."

Later, they used a tape recorder and ran it in the silence and played the tape back again and again, trying to hear voices.

"Did you hear that?" he asked her.

"What? No."

He played it again. The tape hissed and crackled.

"It said, 'Open something,' " he said. " 'Open open open your...' "

They played it again, again, again. Slowly the hisses and crackles started to sound like garbled words. Then less garbled. Then just words.

"Open something..."

"Open," she said. "Open your..."

"Heart," they said together.

"What is the name of that spirit?" he asked her. "Because, I think maybe she wants you to write her story."

"Grace," she said.

Magic

October 17th was supposed to be a cosmic trigger event. Everything was magnified one million times its usual potency.

For this reason, everyone was only supposed to have good thoughts.

Angeli and Mateus and their children danced together in Angeli's living room lit by tangled strings of Christmas lights and the Yom Kippur candles she had not finished burning because she had been afraid to leave them alight all night and hadn't ever lit them again. Angeli and her daughter danced for Mateus and the boys and then Mateus and the boys danced for Angeli and her daughter and then the children each danced alone and then all five of them danced in a circle holding hands. Mateus danced like a punk rocker or a skateboarder, bent over, swinging his arms, gliding his feet and the children did breakdance moves on the floor.

After they danced, they sat under the tree in the garden, on a quilt with prints of running horses, flying birds, flowers and butterflies. It was a warm autumn night with only a slight chill in the air. They ate black beans and rice and tortillas and salad and ice cream. A plane was circling overhead, writing white letters in the sky like clouds. The skywriting read, "Faith."

Because of the astrological significance of the day, they decided to go around in a circle and make some wishes.

Angeli said, "World peace."

Mateus said, "The natural balance is restored."

His son said, "One hundred wishes."

Angeli's son said, "Everybody loves everybody."

Her daughter said, "I wish I could fly."

Mateus said, "Once, we knew how to fly. Everybody knew how to fly. Magic was just part of life. That's what this is about — getting back to the magic."

Then the children got up and danced around the lawn together in the soft autumn twilight. Mateus's arm brushed up against Angeli and she shivered with pleasure. She could feel his warm eyes on her like hands, on her cheek and neck and breasts and between her thighs. She thought, the fact that we are all here together like this, this proves to me that magic is possible, that magic exists.

She watched the children dancing and, if she squinted her eyes, it really looked as if they flew.

Seen

She lay on his bed completely naked and still wet between her legs listening to the sound of a heavy zipper spreading apart thick canvas.

That day, her friend Charlotte had called crying, in the midst of a divorce, saying, "My life is burned to bits. He never saw me. He didn't see who I really was."

Angeli said, "I see who you are. Your true partner will see who you are. It will be easier for him to see you if you clearly see yourself."

Charlotte had said, "Why are you helping me?"

"Because I love you," said Angeli. "You need to be able to see that about yourself, how loveable you are." She wanted to tell Charlotte: Your fragile blond hair washed in silk, your child gymnast's legs doing cartwheels on the street, your arms strong enough to carry a six-year-old wearing the dress you made for her through Manhattan, while wearing on your feet those satin designer platforms as you go off to see another artist, to be their mother, their confidante, their fashion consultant and shrink and wife. "And I'm helping you because I've been there, believe me."

As a child, her father painted her mother again and again, one breast exposed, her long golden hair falling over her shoulders. Once he said, "I paint with my penis." She wished he had not told her this. She wished he had been quiet and painted her portrait, as he had always promised he would. And as an adult she chose a husband who would not see her, who saw porn instead, or huge, dark muscular athletic women who looked nothing like her. This was a way to prove to herself that what she learned to believe as a child (you are unseen) was true.

But this man was different.

She lay on his bed completely naked and still wet between her legs listening to the sound of a heavy zipper spreading apart thick canvas. He took the camera out. Her hands cupped her breasts against the bed and her hips were tilted up slightly, her back arched into the air for him. Outside the window, between black drapes behind white gauze, the city was only dully shimmering lights. There were no traffic sounds because he was playing music, one song after another, each one important to him, each one telling her more about him if she listened carefully.

He had said, "Yesterday, I was so horny all day. I had this erection that wouldn't go away."

On Monday they'd gone to the restaurant with the dark-haired waitresses in tight black jeans and tight black T-shirts who brought you grape leaves and hummus and beer and hookah pipes while you sat under heat lamps in the white lattice patio strung with Christmas lights. She had been afraid, and he had said, "You give me fear, I give you fear. You give me love, I give you love."

She said, "If my child comes to me with fear, I give her love. If my child attacks me with fear, I give him love. If anyone else attacks me with fear, it is harder to give love but if they just reveal their fear, I always try to give them love."

She had started to cry and he said, finally, what she needed to hear. "I just don't want you to be afraid because I love you. We will do whatever it takes."

In his bed that night she had whispered into his ear, "Because you put up with all of that, now you can have anything you want tonight. You can do anything you want."

"You're not afraid?" he asked her.

"No. I am never afraid at all when it comes to sex with you."

She wondered if this exchange had any effect on his endless

Thursday erection. It was Friday and she was already seeing him again, so in a way he had been right, fear spawned more fear and trust and love brought those things. She was not only seeing him again, he was seeing her. He was seeing her with his huge dark eyes through his huge dark camera.

She felt the lens on her loose dark hair, on her downcast, perpetually sad eyes, on her mouth that had not stopped smiling, turned up into a secret, small smile against the pillow. She felt the camera on her small bony shoulders and lean back, her ribcage with each rib delineated, she felt it on her slender, deceptively strong limbs and especially on her ass. He saw asses everywhere—even the line where her thigh met her calf when her legs were bent up under her chin got him hard. She felt the music and the soft light pouring in through all her orifices. It was between her legs and she felt herself coming again, even without him touching her. Just watching her. Seeing who she was. Showing her the woman she now recognized unmistakably, even in her fear, as herself.

Now

Mateus will tell Angeli about a baby he had who died just after her birth. The baby he could not save. At first he believed that the baby did not want to be saved, and later he came to believe that she was not making a conscious choice; she was meant only to come to him briefly and then leave but she was not abandoning him. He will tell Angeli that the baby was, and still is, his angel watching over him. Angeli will recognize, in this account, the lyrics of one of Francisco's songs, also about someone who had died and become his, Francisco's, angel. Mateus will tell her that he knows other angels will come into his life.

Angeli will kiss his face. It will seem so large and rough compared to the tiny, soft faces of her children. (He has told her, "My head is so big! Maybe like those star kids? I wasn't really aware of it until my friends and I were snowboarding and the helmet didn't fit me and then we had this head measuring contest and my head was like two inches bigger than anyone else's!") Her tears will drip onto this large, rough starman face. He will speak to her in Portuguese and she will imagine him as a child without the sideburns and the beard but with the same slow-burning eyes and full, brooding mouth.

She will tell Mateus that she lost two babies as well, though early on, before they were more than a tiny image on the ultrasound screen. But that she loved them and felt their souls leaving her hollow when they went. She will tell him that she wants a child with him, but that it is not necessary. That she could love his star-son with the impossible eyelashes and always neatly trimmed hair the way she loves her own tangled, dusty-footed starchildren, the way she would love a child they had together. The spirit of the babies who died, who chose to go back to their stars instead, will be watching this. They will say, "What is love? Real love is consciousness, nothing more. Now. Now you are awake."

Shaking

I'm at an outdoor concert, dancing near you but you aren't really with me. Your eyes are distant. You shake your hips gracefully, moving sinuously from your pelvis. I remember the first time we danced together. We hadn't made love yet. The tension was so great you wouldn't let my body rub up against yours. But also you never looked away.

The woman approaches, predatory, focused. She is about my age and body type with straight dark hair and tight white jeans, a white camisole, something I would wear, though tonight I'm in a pink and gold lace top and a silky skirt.

I have been advised when another woman tries to hit on your man, gently touch his arm, remind him you are there. I want to run away but instead I make myself put my hand gently on your back. You ignore my touch. It's as if you can't feel me at all. You keep dancing and the woman keeps shaking her ass in your face. I walk away.

Later I return and she is still dancing near you, chatting, asking you questions. I try again to let you both know I am here with you, your girlfriend. I thought I was your girlfriend. We have been making love once a week, though only that, and I'm always the one who calls, for a year. You have told me you love me and that you have never felt so close to anyone. I watch your child for you; you have held my children's hands, gone to their recitals, bought them things. You have taken my photograph to show me myself.

Now you ignore me again. I'm not the girl in the photo, the center of your attention, the picture in your eye. I'm invisible, even in pink and gold lace, even dancing.

I say, "I'm going to go now."

You look at me coldly and say, "Okay. See you later." You do not touch me.

I walk away and stop. The Brazilian music is like flames leaping around me. There is a singed smell but I realize it is coming from inside my body. My girlfriends hold me while I shake and sob. No one can hear me because the music is so loud. It is both my protection and my attacker.

I am crying too hard but it isn't just because of what just happened. There are other things happening. Between us. Not about us. Or not directly. Like the fact that I've already given notice and the loan might not go through on the little yellow cottage I'm trying to purchase, the little house with the roses in front and the mermaid bathroom and the pond. I'm worried that I may not have a place to live. You're worried that I'm going to ask you to move in with me. But that moment when you won't acknowledge me holds in it all the loss of what we have had, a hundred love poems sent to you, unanswered. My sacred dances for your pleasure but not as your partner. The rooms lit with candles where you never came while looking at my face, always from behind. The way you never introduced me to your friends and pretended to everyone that we were not moaning and shaken with love the night before.

In a hospital your wife is pregnant with another man's baby. She is young and beautiful and left you suddenly. You have kept me a secret from her, too. When we first were together you called her your ex but when I got divorced you said, "Congratulations. I still haven't done that." When I asked you why, you explained it was financial. She wants the divorce but she told you that she also wants her new son to have your last name along with his father's.

The gorgeous Brazilian singer with her long braids and bright colors has a voice like ripe, sun-warmed fruit and the drums are in my heart but none of it is beautiful anymore. Nothing is over yet, not for a month or so, but I know I will never see that country where I dreamed we might go to see your family and dance together in the streets.

Not even here, in this city where I was born and will die, not even here can we dance together.

After I calm down, I start to leave with my friends and I see you. I go over and hug you, trying to be loving, trying to be mature. You hold me at arm's distance after a moment. "I thought you left," you say, so cool.

We make love the next night but I don't say a thing about what happened. I wait four days, talk to my therapist. Then I call and ask, "If we are out together and someone hits on either of us, will you put your arm around me to let them know we are together?"

You say "I don't have a problem with that." But when I bring up the woman at the concert you say, "I know she was hitting on me. I know you were upset. I didn't want to deal with it. Besides, after you left, she told me 'I'm going to go meet my boyfriend now.' "

This is said to make me feel relieved—she had a boyfriend and wouldn't have really taken it farther with you. But it makes me feel worse. How did it get to the point that she even told you about her boyfriend, that she even needed to let you know she wouldn't be going home with you? It really shouldn't have been a question. I was with you. Or was I? We didn't come together.

In bed or out, we rarely do.

But three weeks later we are in the gurgling, twinkling backyard of my little yellow dream house where we made love once on the lawn and talked about making love in every room and you are telling me you need space, you like your independence, you don't want a girlfriend. We had something great but it's not working now.

I am crying and sobbing on the step in my garden. I say, "Tell me something, please, give me something."

You only once told me I was beautiful, when I begged you. You said, "You really need validation, don't you?"

Now you say, "You're beautiful. You're an amazing person. People love you. It's breaking my heart to see you like that. Maybe I'm stupid."

For that moment, I feel the love you had for me. Then it's gone. You are talking about us in the past tense again.

I know you want to leave. I put my hand on your leg. I say, "Go now. You can go." And you slip back through my new house, out my front door and into your car, quick and quiet as a black cat. I wonder if you can still hear my sobs from the street.

It's just like a dance, isn't it? This dancing toward each other, coming together shaking with life and desire, this union, this farewell, this standing alone in the darkness gazing out over the crowd to the brightly lit stage where the beautiful woman sings our dreams and then they are gone, she's gone, the night is completely silent. And still.

For a moment I have forgotten all the blessings of my life. My children teaching me the definition of god and goddess every day. My friends with their poems and cakes holding me in their circle of light. My books that have made people cry and fall in love. My little yellow house with the roses and the lily pond.

I am alone with the spirits again. None of them telling me to open my heart now. Not even the one I call Grace, the one who went to Brazil to heal and died anyway. They are quiet, omnipresent, listening to me weep.